All the Fun of the Fair

. . . they could hear the shouting and smashing . . . The sound was terrible – like a massacre. Their voices were hoarse with insult and what they were yelling made her shudder. Then she saw them under the light of the jaundiced moon, gathered around the Gallopers. At first she could not believe what she was seeing, then she began to scream, bellowing in Imran's face . . .

Other books by Anthony Masters

Badger
Streetwise
Cat Burglars (Starling Point Series)

STARLING POINT — 2

All the Fun of the Fair

Anthony Masters

Teens · Mandarin

Acknowledgement

Advice to Young Children
From THE COLLECTED POEMS OF STEVIE SMITH (Penguin Modern Classics) reprinted by permission of James MacGibbon

A Teens · Mandarin Paperback

ALL THE FUN OF THE FAIR

First published in Great Britain 1989
by Teens · Mandarin
Michelin House, 81 Fulham Road, London SW3 6RB
Mandarin is an imprint of the Octopus Publishing Group

British Library Cataloguing in Publication Data
Masters, Anthony
All the fun of the fair
I. Title II. series
823'.914 [F]

ISBN 0–416–12612–X

Printed in Great Britain
by Cox and Wyman Ltd, Reading, Berks

To Robina, Mark, Vicky and Simon with much love and also to Diane Fisk with many thanks for all her research.

One

'I'm not staying round to be treated like a kid!'

Life had been good while Dad was away and now he was back sixteen-year-old Leroy wasn't prepared to be ordered about. Winston, his eleven-year-old brother, gloomily buried himself in the television, shutting out everything else. Mum was in the kitchen, crying and trying to wash the dishes at the same time. In the next room, Gran lay bedridden, listening to the row, grieving for Leroy.

He went out, slamming the door, and ran across the square. Nothing would induce him to go back – not even Mum. Or Winston. Without Dad, he'd been the head of the house, although he'd often had to compete with Gran. But since Dad's return months ago, life had become impossible. He had to be in by eleven at the weekends, go to bed on weekdays at ten, do jobs around the house for nothing, and tonight, because he had been drinking, Dad had hit him. Not hard. But enough to make up his mind. So now he was going. And it was final. Only problem was – where to go?

* * *

Jim North drove the big truck slowly through the early morning streets of South London. The September Fair at Starling Point was one of his best bookings and he was hoping it would rebuild his fortunes – or at least make a contribution.

'Let's hope the punters give us a break,' said his wife Gwen, exactly echoing his thoughts. 'And Derek pulls his weight,' she added. She cast a gloomy eye over the urban wilderness around them. In the old days they had worked the country fairs, but now they didn't have enough money to travel far.

'I like Starling,' said Dan.

'Why can't we go down the seaside?' wailed Sal. The twins were coming up to six now and for the first time were beginning to bicker.

'Seaside's boring.'

'Starling's boring – nothing to do.'

'Shut up, you two,' yelled Gwen and they subsided, too tired to make a real go of a quarrel.

'He's not been too bad lately,' muttered Jim. Derek was his brother-in-law and his partner. He was travelling behind them, driving the van.

'He's a slob,' said Gwen. 'I know – I'm his sister. He's never changed. Comes from a household of women who made life too easy for him.'

Jim often wondered what she meant by that. The household of women had been her and her mum; her dad had walked out when Derek was born. But now Gwen didn't seem to want to admit that she was partly responsible for her brother's upbringing.

'Good mechanic though,' said Jim mildly.

'We could get another.'

'Where?'

It was a conversation they had had a thousand times – and a daydream that haunted them continuously. Whatever his faults, Derek was a brilliant mechanic. Although Jim knew a bit, Derek was a natural.

'We could train someone,' said Gwen.

Jim nodded. Let her dream away – it took the anger out of her.

The Gallopers had been in the family for three generations now: Jim's grandfather, his father, and now him and Derek. Two years ago they had completely restored the ride and it was resplendant in a livery of red and gold and white. Red for the horses' harness, gold for their manes and white for their bodies. They had also rebuilt the steam organ that ground out the tunes for the roundabout horses – the Gallopers – the most famous ride in the business. But the refurbishment had cost money, too much money, and business had been bad ever since. They just weren't getting the bookings. The punters were going for the spectacular rides – the Moon-Shot, Orbiter, Supertrouper, Matterhorn – and now the future was in question for, if the takings did not improve, they would be forced to sell the ride to the highest bidder.

The familiar vast landscape of Starling Point loomed up through the strands of mist that were slowly lifting from the streets. As Jim edged the truck down the service road that led to the main square, Leroy watched from the back seat of an abandoned car. It was the only place he had found to spend the night and he had woken stiff and cold and hungry. But as he stared at the sign on the truck – NORTH AND WINGATE'S WORLD FAMOUS GALLOPERS – he had a sudden inspiration.

Jim and Derek had taken Gallopers to Starling Point for five years now, ever since the September Fair had begun. On the whole it had been trouble free. Despite the many architectural drawbacks of Starling Point and the continuous petty crime committed by some of the younger members of the community, the residents of Starling Point certainly knew how to enjoy themselves. The fair was packed for the few days it lasted and trouble had been limited to a few drunks and kids trying to get free rides. Gallopers was only a part of the fair; the rest of the rides and stalls came in from all over the place.

Starling Point had been built in the sixties, and ugly stains now ran down the sides of the concrete buildings. The flats surrounded a central square and rose to a height of eight interconnected storeys. At each corner there was a medium-sized tower block: a great jagged finger of concrete, twelve storeys tall, pointing menacingly at the sky. The square had shops that were built into the flats but not all had flourished and some were boarded up. There was a fountain in the centre of the square, but where silver water had briefly cascaded there was now a sea of refuse. Below the flats was the underground car park and on a lower floor, leading away from the square, was a youth club, an old people's home, a day centre, a crèche, the welfare office and a job centre. Jim reckoned that you could be born in Starling Point and die in Starling Point; a whole life could be lived there, using the clubs and agencies. Only an undertaker's parlour was missing.

Looking down on the square from the top storey of the tower block was like looking into a vast dry well in which Lilliputian residents darted this way and that, seemingly aimless in their architect-designed prison. Somewhere else, the architects and planners lived in restored town houses, cottages, spick and span private estates: anywhere but near the sterility they had created.

Jim had always reckoned that the inhabitants of Starling Point should, theoretically, have felt trapped and isolated, fearful in the graffiti-decorated passageways and urine-scented lifts. Yet for all that, the whole rambling structure exuded a life and vitality that was not found in the streets around it. Ill-conceived, badly built and battle scarred, Starling Point was a world of its own, but not in quite the way the planners had intended. It was like a battered old ferry, riding out the choppy seas, jammed with anarchistic passengers, fighting, bickering, laughing and living out their plight together.

'Mister.'

Jim was sitting on the steps of the truck, waiting for Derek to arrive with the van and the trailer. He looked at his watch. 10 a.m. It was a wonderful

Indian Summer of a morning and he could have done with a mug of strong black tea. He felt exhausted and now there was this kid bothering him.

'Yeah?'

'Got a job?'

'Nope.'

'OK.' Leroy stepped back, his enthusiasm blunted. The night in the car had been grim but his sudden inspiration had given him hope. Now the hope drained away.

'Mister – '

'Look, sonny, stop bothering me.'

Gwen got out of the truck with the twins. The travelling life suited them; nothing was ever boring and, except for the time they spent in the big yard that was their winter quarters, they saw a new town or village at least twice a week.

'Who's this?'

'A kid who wants a job.'

'Don't you go to school, son?'

'Left,' Leroy said.

'Where do you live?' she persisted.

He gave a vague wave of the hand to one of the tower blocks.

'Does your mum know you're looking for a job?'

'Yes.'

Gwen gave Leroy an sharp look. 'Sure?' She had known many kids who had run away from home and had romantic notions of joining a fair. She was sure this was another one of them.

'We can't give you a job, son,' said Jim. 'No chance. Besides, we're only here a few days.'

'I could go wherever you go.' Leroy sounded childishly plaintive. 'I'd do anything. Any dirty job.'

'You been sleeping rough, haven't you, son?' said Gwen. 'I know the look.'

He hesitated. Should he come clean with them or not? 'Yes.'

'Run away from home?'

'My dad's back. He was inside. I can't live with him.' Leroy spoke with such sincerity that Gwen was moved.

'What about your mum? She'll be sick with worry.'

'Mm.'

'Got any brothers – or sisters?'

'Winston.'

'He'll be upset too.'

'Yeah.'

'You prepared to have your keep for three days and work for peanuts?'

Leroy's eyes brightened. 'You bet.'

Jim groaned. 'Not another lame duck,' he muttered. But Gwen ignored him.

'All right, son. But there's a condition.'

'What's that?'

'You tell your mum where you are.'

'I've run away,' he said indignantly.

'Either you tell her – or you don't work on the ride.'

Leroy thought long and hard while Gwen watched him, the twins played with a ball on the broken concrete of the square and Jim cursed. Gwen was too soft. And where was Derek and the caravan? Where was his tea?

Leroy came back with a compromise.

'If I make out good, can I stay?'

'We'll see. Now go and tell your mum.'

'Thanks.' Leroy sped off.

Jim groaned again. 'Gwen, one of these days . . .'

'All right,' she snapped. 'I'll get your tea.'

'Mum.'

'Leroy!'

She flung her arms round him in the small kitchen but kept talking in a whisper.

'Look, I'm not back. I've just come to tell you I've got a job. For the weekend anyway.'

'Where you got this job?'

'On the roundabout. Down below.'

'The fair?'

'Yeah.'

'That'll be no good. Where you going to sleep?'

That was one thing Leroy hadn't asked. Maybe they would let him sleep under the truck, or even in the truck.

'What you going to do on Monday, son?'

'I don't know. Go with the fair maybe. I'll have a job. I can bring you money, Mum.'

'And what do you think your father's going to say?'

'I don't care what he says. I want to get away from him.'

'He's a good man. He just doesn't know how to cope now he's back home. And especially, he doesn't know how to cope with you. Can't you . . .'

'Give him another chance? No way, Mum. I'm up to here with it.' They were still whispering, growing angrier and angrier every moment.

'You'll miss your schooling.'

'Who cares?' He went to the door.

'Wait!'

'What for?'

'He was upset last night, your dad. He went looking for you.'

'He couldn't have looked very far.'

'Well, he was out for an hour.'

'Some search.'

'And he came back and waited up half the night.'

'So now he's in bed, having a good kip.'

'I *know* he's not easy – '

'Look, Mum, I've got to go. I'll drop back when I can.' Leroy kissed her. 'I love you, Mum,' he said as he ran out of the door.

Gran began to knock on the wall.

'Yes, darling?'

'Don't darling me. Something's up if you call me darling.'

Edna James stood contemplating her mother-in-law who had come to join them from Jamaica about six years ago. Her immigration had not been a success. She didn't like the climate, the country, the house and the fact that, for most of the time, her son Sebastian had been in prison. As a result she had taken to her bed and declared herself an invalid. But she was a very active invalid. And a very dominating one.

'Now you tell me, what's going on?'

'Nothing.'

Verity James drew herself up in bed, her wizened face puckering in anger. 'Don't give me that.'

'Everything's OK,' Edna insisted.

'There's been a row.'

'No.'

'Leroy's walked out.'

'He's looking for a job.'

'And it's Seb's fault.'

'They were having a talk.'

'A row.'

'They got a bit heated.'

'Seb kicked him out.'

Edna finally gave in. 'All right, Verity,' she snapped, 'if you know what happened, why ask?'

The old lady's deep-set eyes were lit up with malicious pleasure. She loved scoring off her daughter-in-law. It was a temporary triumph – a source of elation in a deadly dull world.

'Send Seb in.'

'He's gone out.'

'If that boy of mine had been taken in hand when you married him, he'd never have gone inside that jail.'

Edna sighed. It was a familiar tack. The implication was that Verity would have kept him out of jail and that Edna had practically thrown him in. She looked out of the window as her mother-in-law's voice rose and fell. Despite all the problems – and there were certainly plenty of them – she loved the community at Starling Point and had come to rely on it. Soon she would nip down to her friend Virginia and pour out her troubles. That was the good thing about the estate: there was always someone near. Someone to pop in to. If she hadn't been able to do that she would have gone barmy.

'Must go.'

'No more darling, eh?'

'I've got Winston's lunch to get.'

'Don't bother about me.'

'I'm going to make you something nice.'

'What's something?'

'Nice plate of hot-pot.'

'All that Jamaican stuff. Why don't you eat British?'

'Haddock,' said Edna, knowing that Verity hated British food and was just trying to annoy her.

'Can't stand the stuff. Mark my words – '

But Edna didn't, hurriedly leaving the room.

Winston arrived home at lunchtime, still wearing his football kit. Edna was too late to stop him running over the carpet, leaving a trail of muddy prints.

'Look at that filthy mess. Why didn't you – '

Winston ignored her.

'Where's Dad? And is Leroy back?'

'Your dad's down the boozer – and Leroy's got himself a job.'

'Job?'
'On the fair.'
'Blimey. You let him?'
'He's grown up now.'
'Can I work on the fair when I'm grown up?'
'Fair? What's this about a fair?' Gran's thin, sharp voice came from behind her closed door.
'She's got X-ray ears,' said Winston. 'Hears what's happening in Kingston, Jamaica.'
'Shh.'
'What's that?' Gran's voice was even sharper. 'And where's my lunch?'
Edna fled, leaving Winston to head for his bedroom, spreading more mud as he went.

'Here comes trouble.'
By this time the van and trailer had arrived and Jim North was at last drinking his tea. Sitting on the step beside him was his brother-in-law Derek. He'd been working with Jim since he was a kid and he was now in his early thirties – a huge thickset man who wasn't very bright and whose sole interest was machinery. Several times Jim, who was tall and thin and wiry and no match for Derek, had tried to get rid of him, but the ride had so many mechanical problems these days that Derek was becoming more and more necessary. The problem was that he was lazy and unreliable and showed no signs of improvement.
'Trouble?' said Derek. 'I should say so.'
Coming into the square was another truck, this

time much more down at heel, with faded lettering and a good number of dents in the bodywork. They could just make out the words: GERRY KITSON'S MYSTERY RIDE. IT'S THE DANGER ZONE!

'Danger zone is dead right,' muttered Jim. 'I can't see why that guy's still on the road. The Guild have threatened to take his card away. You know he used to be a scrap metal dealer, and his father before him. And that's all that ride is.'

'You've always had your knife into him,' said Derek. 'What he does is none of our business.'

'The guy makes it everyone's business. He gives us all a bad name.'

'Mister.'

'Who's this kid?' Derek's gravelly voice and bulk made Leroy uneasy.

'Oh him. My wife's lame duck. Gwen!' he bellowed.

She emerged from the caravan with one of the twins squealing behind her.

'What's your name again?'

She hadn't asked him. 'Leroy,' he said.

'Come in.'

Once in the caravan he was amazed. It was like a palace, with shining chrome and mirrors, china arranged in gleaming cabinets, coloured photographs of the children and fairground families on the wall, gleaming brass, and a miniature barrel organ on the mantelpiece.

'You'll have to prove yourself.'

Leroy sat down gingerly on a chintz-covered sofa.

'Who to?'

'Me, of course.' She smiled at him. 'But particularly Jim and Derek.'

'I'm strong.'

'You'll need to be.'

'What have I got to do?'

'Help set up. Then wash and polish the Gallopers for a start.'

'Then what?'

'When we open you can take the tickets – save Derek a job. You've got to make sure you take the right money.'

It sounded simple enough.

'Why don't you get on with your dad, son?'

She was going to pry. He knew it.

'Do I have to talk about it?'

'No.'

'I can do the job.'

'We'll see.'

'And if I prove myself?'

'We'll see,' she said again.

There was a pause.

'One thing – '

'Yes?'

'Where're you going to sleep tonight, son?'

'Don't know.'

'Then you sleep on the floor in the truck. I'll give you a mattress and some blankets.'

I thought she'd never ask, thought Leroy with relief.

Two

By that evening Gallopers was up and running. So was Gerry Kitson's Mystery Ride as well as a number of other rides and sideshows that had arrived in the day. There was the Big Wheel, Dodgems, Slammer and Orbiter as well as Shooters, Picks, Darts and Candy Floss and Hot Dogs.

Leroy had never felt so tired in his life. He had helped Jim and Derek level the centre, put in the swift and rafters from which the Gallopers hung, then the centre and running board. He was exhausted. But he was happy. It was a different world. He had crossed this square a million times, but the fairground had given it another life. With its garish lights and oily smells, it was a mechanical carnival, timeless and exotic.

Now he was balancing on the swaying platform where the horses stood. He tried to collect the money when the ride was moving slowly, but this was not always possible and, by the time he had collected from every punter, the Gallopers were racing and Leroy had to use all his agility to keep his balance. Luckily he was strong and well co-ordinated so he managed not to fall off. It would have been great fun, but all the time he was conscious of the indifference of Jim and Derek. They largely ignored him now, although he had received plenty of impatient instructions during the set-up. He realised that in their eyes he was a useless kid. It was only Gwen who had encouraged him with mugs of tea and the occasional wink. She was a big, comfortable woman with a large bust and hips; she easily dominated the men, sailing round like a huge galleon. The twins were friendly as well and he played with them in his few breaks. He was fed bacon sandwiches and corned beef hash so he didn't go hungry. But as the hours passed, he began to miss Mum and Winston very much indeed and the missing soon became a sharpening pain, dimming the pleasure he had felt in his new-found glorious freedom.

The atmosphere was heady though. The tinsel lights, the steam organs and disco music, the gaudy atmosphere of the fair bathed the square in an alien light and the tower blocks became castle ramparts. Hundreds of people had turned out and there was a good feeling of frantic happiness. Everyone had put their troubles behind them for the evening.

Gallica, Imran and Sharon had done exactly that. Saving up their enjoyment, they had tried most of the other rides by the time they finally arrived at Gerry Kitson's Mystery Ride. It looked the best ride in the whole fair, with its twin columns and mysterious snaking tunnel. The fact that some of the canvas was torn and the lettering had peeled off didn't worry them in the least.

They never really understood exactly what happened. The three of them started off in one car and there seemed to be five other cars close behind them. In pitch darkness, broken by sudden bursts of flashlight, they careered over a track that ran up and down one tower, along the tunnel and up and down the other tower. The ride was accompanied by banshee wails, coffins opening, dismembered corpses, skeletons, bats, werewolves and vampires, dripping blood, appearing from cupboards. They screamed and yelled, concealing their slight disappointment. The cars went fast and were breath stopping, but the effects were very amateur. Then, on the second tower, it all went tragically wrong.

They were on top of the switchback when something seemed to lock the wheels of the front car carrying Gallica, Sharon and Imran. The following car hit theirs and then fell back on the other four, forcing them backwards. The car that was in the rear left the rails and with a terrible rending, clattering, screaming sound plunged into the darkness. The cries of the injured and the hysterical screams of those who were still on the track made the darkness an inferno of terror.

'Don't move a muscle,' said Gallica, 'or we're going to be off the track and down there.' She shut her eyes, but what she imagined was much worse. When she opened them again all she could see was a velvet darkness. The groaning and whimpering of the injured was appalling. Gallica's thoughts turned to her parents and how her death would probably kill them, too. They had only been in England two years and the great plains of Zimbabwe they had left behind made it very difficult for them to settle into the confines of Starling Point. Their love for each other had kept them going, but it was not until a few months ago that they had begun to regard England as home and, from her point of view, much of that had to do with her friendship with Imran and Sharon. She looked at them now in the front of the car, their arms locked round each other. She wished there was someone to cuddle her, to protect her against the painful darkness. As if realising this, Sharon put her hand gently behind her and Gallica took it gratefully.

'Don't *move*,' hissed Imran. His presence comforted her too, dousing the rising panic that kept swelling up inside her. He was tall and dark and resourceful-looking. Sometimes she resented his managing air; now she needed it desperately. Next year Imran was meant to be going to the Pakistan Military Academy: a grinding bone of contention between him and Sharon. Surely a military cadet would know what to do to get them out of here?

'What are we going to do?' Gallica asked him desperately. The screaming was getting worse behind them and there was a terrifying groaning from soneone below.

'If anyone moves we've had it,' said Imran. 'Look how precariously we're balanced.'

They stared down apprehensively. He was dead right.

'Sit tight,' Imran continued. 'Keep still and some-one will come.'

Suddenly their car quivered, moved backwards in a rending of metal – and stopped again. Imran began to pray to Allah as he had not prayed in years.

'Please God,' said Sharon between clenched teeth, 'let it be OK.' She sounded much cooler than she was feeling. Sharon had become so important to Gallica. Whilst in Africa she had imagined London girls to be as hard and as brittle as their brightly varnished nails. But Sharon was warm and loving and if she had a tougher side it was only because of her problems. Her repressive parents were always over-working and her brother Mick was out of work, out of favour, and at odds with Imran. Supposing Sharon was killed and she stayed alive?

The car rocked again and Gallica whimpered, the tears coursing down her cheeks. Sharon tightened her grip on her hand and Imran said softly, 'It's going to be all right if we all sit still.'

The Gallopers slowed to a halt as Jim turned off the steam organ. A crowd had gathered around the Mystery Ride and Gerry had run out of his box office and inside his dilapidated show. A few seconds later he dashed out again, shouting to Derek to get an ambulance. Derek, with surprising agility, leapt off the platform and on to the ground, pounding towards the telephone box on the edge of the square.

Leroy, meanwhile, was watching the rides and sideshows grind to a halt as people left them, rushing towards the grim sound of the screaming. It seemed to echo round the concrete fortress of Starling Point. The full moon was riding high in the sky and clouds tumbled past it, making it look muddy, leprous.

'Hi, son,' The voice was soft.

Leroy looked down and saw his dad.

'What do you want?'

'To make sure you're safe.'

'You came looking – '

'Like I did the other night.' His father's normally set features were softer, less assured. 'I don't want you running away from home.'

'There's trouble over there.'

His father turned round. It was as if he was seeing the crowds for the first time, so single-minded had been his search for Leroy. A longer, sharper scream echoed over the square and Jim and Gwen ran into the crowd towards the Mystery Ride.

'Let's see what we can do,' said Leroy's dad. His huge frame sent the back of the crowd scattering and Leroy ran after him blindly.

'Got any lights, Gerry?'

'They've fused.'

'Flashlight?' asked Jim impatiently. Gerry ran back to the office and produced one.

'What's going on?' asked Leroy's dad.

'The ride's closed,' snapped Gerry. 'We have a small problem to work out.' He looked calm but inside he could feel the panic rising.

'Can we do anything? I'm Sebastian James, this boy's father.'

Jim's reply was lost as the flashlight illuminated the real devastation of the switchback. The cars were hanging half on and half off the soaring gradient of the track, with the front car still on top. The car that had left the track was lying upside down. People were scattered around it, some moaning, others silent. The skeleton framework of the switchback was sheer, more than ten metres high. I could climb that, thought Leroy.

'I could climb that,' said Sebastian.

'Climb it?' Gerry stared at him.

'Yeah. I can get people down.'

'I can't allow it.' Gerry's voice was brusque.

Jim intervened. 'You called the fire brigade, Gerry?'

Gerry stared hopelessly at him.

'I got the ambulance.'

'You bloody fool. We need ladders.'

Gerry burst into angry, stuttering speech but Sebastian shouted him down.

'Look, I can get up there!'

'You a professional climber or something?' Gerry sneered.

'No, but I'm strong.'

'Can I come with you, Dad?'

Sebastian looked across at Leroy for a moment. Then he nodded. 'We'll start with the nearest car. You come up with me and we'll see if we can lever them out so that I can take them down on my back. It'll be a long job.'

'I'll get the fire brigade,' yelled Jim. 'I'm on my way.'

'Be careful, son.' It was Gwen's voice, warm and reassuring. She made Leroy feel that he could do it. But already he was swarming up the fine tracery of metal, finding a foothold here, a foothold there, way behind his father's giant swinging frame. Sebastian climbed like an ape, never doubting where to put a foot or a hand, climbing relentlessly on until he was abreast of the first car.

Leroy hung underneath his father, watching him gently coax a young mother.

'You come on my shoulder, missus. I'll have you down in a few seconds. Directly you're out, my boy will take the kid. You're too heavy for him.'

Somehow she managed to find the courage to cling on to him and Sebastian began to climb down past Leroy. As he inched his way, he said, 'OK, son, you get the kid.'

Leroy climbed on up, and when he came abreast with the car he saw a boy of about eight staring at him with enormous terrified eyes.

'What's your name?'

'Ben.'

'Do you want me to give you a fireman's lift?'

Ben shook his head and then looked up as a violent creaking came from further up the track.

'Come on, Ben,' encouraged Leroy. 'It'll be fun.' He looked down. 'See – your mum's on the ground already. Quite safe.'

'I want her,' whimpered Ben as he held out his arms.

* * *

'Sit *still*,' said Imran. Sharon froze. They had all felt movement in the car again.

'There's a man climbing up,' said Gallica. 'He's lifting people out. There's a kid, too. Pretty good climbers.'

The car moved again and Sharon let out a little moan of fear.

Imran took her hand. 'We'll be OK now,' he said.

'How many cars has he got to go?'

'Two. But the fire brigade will be here soon. They'll have ladders. You don't imagine that guy is all there is, do you?'

Their car swayed again. Sharon closed her eyes. What would death be like? she wondered. What was there after all the hurting?

'I don't like the look of that.'

'Neither do I,' agreed Leroy.

Ben was safely back in the care of his mother and Leroy and his father were looking up at the top car, as it rocked gently and alarmingly.

'We should deal with that one next, son. Think you can make it?'

'You bet I can.'

'Good for you,' said Gwen.

They swarmed up the iron network again, and this time Leroy found it almost easy. He was amazed that his dad was such a good climber, but he was even more amazed that he was actually working with him like this. They were like mates.

When they came alongside the car, Sebastian said, 'Steady now, this one's come off its rails.'

'So will I if I don't get out,' said Sharon, looking down at them, her body rigid in her attempts not to move at all.

'I'm gonna put you over my back, young lady,' said Sebastian.

'If you can lift me, that is.' The more she joked, the more ordinary she felt. And terrible things couldn't happen to ordinary people, could they?

'I'll try. And the young gentleman – I'll come back for you and the other lady.'

'I can climb out,' said Imran, desperate to assert himself now.

'I'd rather you didn't. You've been stuck in one position so long you'll be stiff and your legs might give out.' Sebastian's voice was very authoritative.

'Can't I help, Dad?'

His father looked at him and grinned.

'Want to take the other young lady on your back, son?'

'Sure.'

While Sharon clung to Sebastian, Gallica hauled herself on to Leroy's back and shut her eyes.

'We can't go on meeting like this,' she said and he felt her go limp. She must have passed out, he thought in panic, but then she tightened her grip and wound her legs round his waist. She was heavy, and as his father climbed easily past him he wondered if he could bear her weight. But as he began to descend, he felt more confident and it was only when he reached the ground and deposited her in a heap that Leroy began to shake.

'You all right, son?' asked Sebastian as he started his climb again.

'I'm fine, Dad,' said Leroy. In fact, he wanted to be sick.

The fire brigade arrived a few minutes later, just as Sebastian was cautiously bringing Imran down.

'Who do you think you are?' asked one of the firemen as he set up a ladder. 'Superman?'

'Clark Kent on a good day,' said Sebastian modestly as the sirens continued to scream outside. 'Over to you.'

'If you've left us anything to do,' said a policeman, watching the ladder being run up and a fireman swarming to the second car.

'You lot OK?' asked Leroy.

Gallica, Sharon and Imran watched the injured being taken away and tried to control the trembling that seized their limbs. Sharon's brother Mick, who had been in the crowd, had come over to see if she was all right. An ambulanceman asked them if they needed hospital attention, but none of them were hurt, just considerably shaken up.

'Shock is a funny thing,' said the ambulance man grimly. 'Comes on apace afterwards.'

'Thanks,' said Imran, sitting down heavily.

'You've been fantastic,' said Gallica to Leroy. 'You and your dad.'

Sebastian came up and put his arm round Leroy.

'He's going to say it was nothing,' said Sharon. She

was very close to a mixture of tears and laughter. The ambulance man was still hovering hopefully; he would definitely take her into hospital if she started laughing so she suppressed the wild giggle that was bubbling away inside her. She glanced at Gallica, wondering if she had the same feeling. Did shock really have this kind of effect?

'I've got to go home, son,' said Sebastian. 'Mum will be worried. Will we see you there?' Leroy hesitated and his father added quickly, 'In your own good time,' and strode away without looking back.

Leroy looked around for Jim, but there was no sign of him or of Gerry either. Somewhere in the semi-darkness he saw Gwen helping someone out, with the twins walking slowly and disconsolately behind her. Leroy realised for the first time that any accident in a fairground must be like an accident to a family. Suddenly he felt a touch on his arm. It was Gallica.

'What's your name?' she asked.

'Leroy.'

'And your dad?'

Leroy looked around but he had vanished into the dark space which was now full of searchlights and firemen and ladders.

'Sebastian,' he said slowly.

'Am I going to see you again?'

Leroy suddenly saw how beautiful she was. But he couldn't think of anything to say and was too surprised even to answer her.

'When can I see you again?' she repeated impatiently.

'I work on the Gallopers,' he muttered. 'I'm really busy.'

'The what?'

'The roundabout – with the horses. We call it the Gallopers.' He felt a sudden onrush of warmth as he said 'we'. He was one of the showmen now, and he had helped to rescue this fantastically beautiful girl who was now asking to go out with him.

'So you go round with the fair?' She sounded impressed.

He hesitated, a sudden honesty overcoming him. 'Not exactly. It's my first job.'

'Where do you live?'

'Here – in Starling.'

'So do I. Do you go to the Comprehensive?'

'Used to.'

'Haven't seen you around.' There was a pause. 'Want to see me again?' she asked persistently.

'Sure.' Leroy looked away. What was the matter with him? He wasn't usually this bad with girls. Maybe *he* was suffering from shock.

'When?'

'I'm on the fair for the weekend.' It all seemed so hopeless.

'You lucky devil.' She turned to Sharon and Imran who were sitting on the ground talking quietly. Imran had his arm round Sharon and she was leaning her head on his shoulder. Quickly Gallica turned back to him. 'There must be some time when we can meet,' she said rather sadly.

Leroy was bewildered. He had never met a girl who

had pursued him so forcefully before. But he supposed it was because he had just rescued her. She must be still suffering from shock and he was sure that she would forget about him in the morning. What with the miracle of the job, the sudden appearance of his father and the terrifying climb, Leroy felt very confused.

'Come down here about six,' he said trying – and failing – to sound cool.

'I'll look forward to that,' she said.

Suddenly he wanted to kiss her. Hard. Instead, Leroy turned away from her and pushed his way through the crowd.

As he arrived at the roundabout he bumped into Gwen. Without warning she threw her arms round him and kissed him.

'You and that dad of yours. Heroes, that's what you are!'

'Yeah.' Leroy tried unsuccessfully to disentangle himself from her.

'So you'll be going home tonight?'

'Might do.' He'd already made up his mind that he would but he didn't want her to patronise him.

She looked at him hard, almost angrily. Then she smiled and said nothing.

Leroy was determined not to give anything away. However much he liked Gwen he wasn't going to be treated like a child and give up his new-found independence.

'Can I go on working here?' he asked woodenly.

'You bet,' she said.

Three

Gallica lay on her bed and stared up at the ceiling. She was full of a strange elation. The shock of the accident and the meeting with Leroy had made her feel light-headed, almost drifting. She closed her eyes and smelt Africa. The smell was special: hot and dry and animal. She saw the veldt. It was dry and dusty and there was a lot of scrub grass. Down the dirt track there was a river and it broadened into a cool lake. That was where they used to swim in the evenings. Out in the bush she could just pick out lions and antelope and wildebeeste, and in the heat haze on the dirt road she saw a mirage. It was Leroy. He ran towards her and she took him in her arms, feeling his body, hard and resilient. Her lips closed on his. They were as cool as the lake.

'Cocoa?'

Gallica unwillingly surfaced to see her mother at her bedside with the steaming drink.

'How you feeling?'

'Fine.'

'Drowsy?'

Gallica nodded.

'Drink this and go off to sleep.'

While she sipped at her cocoa, Gallica suddenly asked, 'Do you ever want to go back to Africa?'

'What to?' Her mother sat on the edge of the bed.

'Suppose my cousin died?'

'We'd have a run-down farm.'

'But I'd be an African Queen.'

Her mother laughed. 'And I'd be Queen Mother.'

'But it's true.'

'It's an old tribal title. Means nothing now. You wouldn't want to go back, would you?'

Gallica shook her head. 'I belong here now,' she said. 'But you don't.'

Her mother sighed. 'I yearn for the old country – it's like a pain inside me. So does your dad. It hits us when he's driving a tube and I'm cleaning an office. But I know we can't go back. That farm's run-down . . .'

'You could build it up.'

'We're too old now. Anyway, why all this?'

'I was thinking up there on that awful Mystery Ride. I did a lot of thinking. I thought how much I loved you and Dad – and I was wondering if you were happy.'

'We're happy.' She leant down and kissed Gallica on her milky lips. 'We're happy if you're happy.'

Gallica smiled and slowly drifted off to sleep. She dreamt of the veldt again. This time she was in a tree. Looking down through the dusty, brittle foliage she saw Leroy coming slowly towards her.

* * *

'We could have died.'

'I expect Mick wishes I had.'

'Don't go on about him.'

Imran and Sharon were sitting in the youth club at Starling Point. It was a battered comfortable place with murals on the walls. An artist had helped the local kids paint them. They showed the piazza, the tower blocks, the supermarket that Imran's parents ran, the playground at Starling Comprehensive and other scenes around Starling Point. The murals were peopled by dozens of different nationalities, all shopping, playing, talking, running, jumping, and dancing together. The vibrant colours seemed to bathe the dingy youth club in a radiant light of its own.

Imran's masculinity had been affronted by being carried so ignominiously down the girders. Shocked and exhausted, his mood was grim. As usual, he had her brother Mick in his thoughts and he kept looking at him across the floor in a brooding, menacing way. For weeks now, the situation between the two boys had been getting worse and Sharon felt helpless, as if she was a sailing dinghy, wind-locked between two great battleships who kept pressing nearer. Sometimes she literally felt breathless, squeezed not only between their rivalry but also by her parents' stifling rules and the crushing fact that her father despised his son and Mick was fully, painfully, aware of it. Nothing she or her mother could do had ever compensated for the way he had gradually snuffed out Mick's spirit.

Before she had met Imran, Sharon had been Mick's

close friend and confidante. He had depended on her, seen her as the one strength in his life. But now he was alone.

'I don't like the way he looks at me,' said Imran, still watching Mick, who was playing snooker.

'He's not looking at you,' said Sharon wearily. They had had this conversation so many times before. 'You don't know what it's like for him at home,' she burst out suddenly. 'He's really despised by my parents – and all because he can't get a job.'

Somewhere deep inside him, Imran had to agree that Mick had a raw deal. Mr Newby was a dried-up little stick of a man, who worked for the post office in a white collar job and who served on the community council of Starling Point. He was pompous and narrow and joyless. Mrs Newby worked in a run-down little estate agents' office a few streets away from Starling Point and hated every moment of it. So different from his own home, thought Imran, which was devout and loving. His father ran the local supermarket. He was a profoundly religious man. Imran's younger brother Naveed and his mother Jasmin were also devout; he was the only one who had drifted away from Islam. But although this caused contention it never produced the warfare he saw in so many of the Western families around him.

'Anyway,' said Imran abruptly, anxious to hurt Sharon, to make her love him more, 'I'll be going to the Military Academy soon. You'll never see me again once I'm in Pakistan. Then you and your precious Mick can be together.'

Sharon sighed, the much-repeated agony moving in her like a knife. But she knew why he did it. Imran had got to a stage where the East and the West had collided in his life and he didn't know how to handle it. She leant over and tried to kiss him but he pushed her away and stood up.

'I'm going home to get some kip,' he said and walked out of the club.

Sharon sat on her own until Mick came up.

'Want to go down the chippy?'

'No.'

'I saw he'd gone. Thought you might need some company.'

'No thanks,' said Sharon. She pushed past him and hurried into the ladies.

Leroy opened the door of the flat very tentatively. He paused in the hall, suddenly shy, unable to face the father he had condemned for so long, not knowing how to handle him now that he was friendly and loving. Leroy felt thoroughly confused and also incredibly tired. He could hear the low drone of the television set and something else that at first he could not identify. Then he remembered what it was – the sound of his father snoring.

He opened the door of the living room. The sight was familiar enough. Winston was on the floor, flat on his stomach with his legs kicking an armchair. Mum was in her chair with a cup of tea and Dad was flat out on the sofa. So many times Leroy had regarded the scene with boredom and had rushed off to a mate's house or to football training. But this time he saw the living room as a sanctuary.

Mum looked up and smiled at him. 'You're a hero, boy,' she said and Winston did something no one could have believed possible. He switched off the television, stood up and then ran at Leroy and punched him on the shoulder.

'You were great, man. Will you be on the telly?'

Then Dad woke up. He rubbed his eyes blearily and said, 'Come here, son.'

Leroy went over and sat on the floor beside him.

'It's been hard since I came out and I ain't treated you right,' said Sebastian awkwardly. 'But you couldn't know what it was like to be inside, to realise what a mess I'd made of it all. Then when I came out – well, you'd pretty well grown up without me and I couldn't handle it.'

Leroy heard a noise from Mum's chair. Then he realised she was crying.

'So I'm going to make amends,' said his dad. 'I know I got a lot to make up to you.'

'It's all right, Dad,' said Leroy, almost fiercely. 'It's all right.'

Mick looked at his watch. It was just after midnight. The fair had closed at eleven and there were only a few security lights left on. The clouds had covered the moon and as he crossed the central square few people passed him. There were no pubs on the Starling Point complex, but the surrounding South London streets were full of them and Mick had already had a skinful. He had a key to the front door and planned to creep in later, go to bed and sleep well into the next morning. Life on the dole was so boring and predictable that he tried to drink as much as he could afford each evening so he could sleep. He would wake at midday and only have the fag end of the afternoon to live through before going to the youth club and then the pub. The only exception to this routine were his visits to an old lady he had strangely befriended and Thursdays, when he had to visit the Job Centre. It was not that he hadn't tried to get work, he had. But with his lousy academic record and lack of any training there wasn't much going. The only job he'd actually tried was in a slaughter-house – and he'd left it after a couple of days. Not only were the working conditions appalling but the pay was so low it was just about the same as he would get on the dole.

Life was grim. In the past, Sharon had always alleviated his misery with her companionship and support, but since she had been going with Imran she hadn't had time for him. Mick was bitterly resentful. He felt nothing for his parents now and only regarded the flat as a place where he could sleep and escape into the telly in the afternoons.

Mick walked the streets once the pubs were shut. He was a tall, strongly built boy and had little fear of muggers. He knew that if he didn't exhaust himself he would never sleep.

He saw the figure in front give a slight stagger and almost fall. He recovered himself but leant against a wall and nursed his ankle. As Mick strolled on he saw the man was quite young with a shock of blond hair and a deeply tanned, almost leathery face that looked nearly black in the now moonless night. Then he recognised him. It was the bloke who ran the Mystery Ride. Mick grinned as he remembered Imran being carried helplessly down the metal skeleton.

'Wotcher.'

The man stared at him in surprise and then began to walk hurriedly on. Mick knew that he had been drinking. I could mug him, he thought. But he knew he wouldn't. Years ago he had pinched some fags from a supermarket and had been easily caught, getting away with a warning from the Juvenile Bureau. This had been the beginning of the end with his parents. Then another idea flashed into Mick's mind.

'Hang on,' he said.

'Yeah?' The man turned round suspiciously.

'Don't I know you?'

'Do you?' He began to walk on again but Mick kept pace with him.

'Aren't you the bloke who runs the Mystery Ride? You had an accident tonight, didn't you?'

'Bit of technical trouble.' Gerry Kitson glanced at the distance between the square where he was now standing and his trailer. Drunk or not, Gerry reckoned he could run for it.

'Want anyone to give you a hand?'

'What with?' His voice was hostile now.

'Clearing up? Bit of repair work?'

'I got staff.' Gerry paused. The alcohol in his body had been giving him one obsessive thought for the last hour. A mental image of Jim North was burnt into his consciousness. The accident would get him closed down sure enough but Jim would put the boot in for him with the Guild to such an extent that he might get closed down for ever. He had already spent hours mentally rehearsing the conversation Jim would be having with the Guild's safety blokes. Suddenly, Gerry's hatred crystallised and he beamed poisonously at Mick.

'You got a job?'

'I'm on the dole.'

'There *is* something you could do for me.'

'Bit of ready in it?'

'Could be. Want to have a talk in my trailer?'

Mick shrugged and then followed him suspiciously.

Jim and Gwen lay in bed, the twins peacefully asleep below them.

'That should fix him.'

'Gerry?' she murmured. 'I wouldn't be so sure.'

'The Guild'll close him. I phoned to make sure.'

'You've made an enemy there, Jim. He's bound to guess you had a hand in it. You've never left him in much doubt about your attitude.'

'Doesn't worry me. He's a menace. Those punters could have been killed. I can't stand by and see safety rules broken, Gwen. Not like that – as if they just didn't matter. His run of luck is over.'

She took his hand. 'Most people would just turn a blind eye.'

They were silent. Then Jim said, 'Lousy night's take.'

'You sure that Derek's pulling his weight?'

'You should know. He's your brother.'

'Do we need him?'

'You know we need him.'

'What about that kid?'

'Leroy? He's a schoolboy. And what about his family?'

'After what his dad did – '

'I know.'

She was silent for a while.

'Or someone like him?'

'A strong kid? We need someone with experience. You know that. Why you suddenly so against Derek?'

'Because he's a fat slob,' she said quietly. 'Always was – and I don't trust him. He's got something on his mind. Something nasty. Know who I saw him talking to before that happened? All excited like.' Her voice was shrill.

'Who?'

'Gerry.'

'Well?'

'It's not healthy, is it?'

'Those two always had a bit in common – the boozer, for instance.'

'There's more than that.' She turned away from him and closed her eyes. 'He's up to something, Jim.'

* * *

By the time Mick had had a large whisky he was not only agreeing to what Gerry was asking him but was also beginning to pour out his grievances. On his second whisky he told Gerry all about Sharon and Imran and how they had ganged up on him. Gerry listened sympathetically but gently returned Mick to the subject in hand.

'So you reckon you can help me, do you?'

'Sure.'

Gerry was sceptical. He could trust no one and although the meeting with Mick had given him a sudden idea it was now making him uneasy. It had been difficult enough to face what had happened just when he was taking on a new partner, yet alone exploring the possibility of taking on the dubious-looking Mick. But his instinct for revenge was strong – and it was fortified by the massive dose of alcohol he had just consumed.

It was only four years ago that Gerry, then twenty-six, had struck out and thrown off the influence of his domineering Irish parents. Originally tinkers, they now owned a big scrap-yard in Surrey and Gerry, their only son, had been their appointed heir. But he had grown to hate the unwieldy piles of metal and the hard-bargaining dealers he had to meet every day. His parents were roughly kind, his sisters warm-hearted, the job lucrative, but he wanted better. Although he left school hardly able to read, Gerry had mechanical skills, particularly with metal, and by building the Mystery Ride he had finally been released from the clutches of his family. Unfortunately his skills, although good, were not up to such a mechanical feat and the ride broke down time after time, culminating in the accident. He had already had warnings from the Guild. They regularly inspected the rides and, although he had made the repairs they wanted and therefore retained the ticket without which no fair would book him, he had to face the fact that the Mystery Ride was now finished. Gerry switched off the thoughts. Whatever happened he was not going back to the yard. Back to his triumphant parents. Whatever happened.

Mick's head drooped on the table and Gerry returned abruptly to present concerns.

'Time to go home, me old son.'

'Haven't got a home.'

The maudlin stage, thought Gerry. I've kept him too long. I'll have to get rid of him somehow. I don't want Jim North to see him in the morning.

'Up!' he said a good deal less gently and Mick tried and failed. He slumped down again and Gerry was forced to help him to his feet. Eventually he managed to propel Mick to the door and with a steadying hand helped him down the steps of the caravan.

'Home, boy.'

He watched Mick sway across the square. But he reckoned it had been worth it. The call from the Guild had come quickly, just a couple of hours ago, and he knew that it was Jim who had shopped him. After all, he had repeatedly warned him that he would.

Gerry turned to the Gallopers, dark and still in the moonlight. He could just make out their noble wooden heads. He was sure they were laughing at him.

Four

The Urban Farm was tucked away on an old railway siding just behind Starling Point. Gallica had gone there at first as a volunteer, but she was now given some pocket money each week to feed the sheep and goats and chickens and pigs that inhabited the narrow strip of land.

On summer evenings she would hurry home, grab some tea and then get into some old clothes. Later, when they had fed and bedded down the animals, she would sit with some of the other helpers and talk while the light slowly faded over the scrubby grass of the old railway embankment and track. Sometimes she would walk down its short length, consumed by her own thoughts.

Nature had reclaimed the old track in a tangle of bushes, heady-smelling wild flowers and a narrow path. This Saturday afternoon she was thinking of Leroy. Gallica had woken up feeling good, with no aftereffects from the day before. All she could think about was the dramatic rescue and Leroy's face appearing over the edge of the car. Each moment she longed for six o'clock as she sat amongst the sweet-scented grasses. The pain was a yearning but there was a sharpness to it. There was also another growing feeling inside her: a desire to touch his body. She was almost frightened and knew that she had never experienced this sensation so strongly before. Gallica picked up a dandelion clock and began to blow at it. He loves me. He loves me not. He loves me . . .

The fair was due to open at five. Leroy had spent the morning cleaning the Gallopers and the afternoon at home sleeping. He was now ready to start work. He hadn't said much to his dad. The great joy was that there was a kind of contented silence which did not have to be broken. But as he approached Jim's trailer his mood was shaken for, from inside, came the sound of raised angry voices. Vaguely he wondered what was going on.

But Leroy's thoughts soon returned to the romantic changes that had occurred in his life. The suddenness of his job on the Gallopers, the accident to the Mystery Ride and, as a result of that, the new relationships with his father and Gallica. He felt muddled, insecure, punch-drunk by the pace of events and his conflicting loyalties to Gallopers – and to Gallica. Gallopers and Gallica, the words rang an insistent rhythm in his mind, and to avoid reality Leroy took grateful refuge in fantasy. He would work on the fair when he left school and have his own ride. He would have a smart trailer in which he and Gallica would live contentedly. They would have lots of children and live happily ever after. Leroy daydreamed on as he gave the Gallopers a final proud wipe and polish.

'I just don't believe it!' yelled Jim.

He was confronting Derek over the polished window table. Gwen listened in the kitchen, fearful of violence. The twins were playing behind the ride somewhere and she was grateful for that, at least.

'Give the guy a break. You've been witch-hunting him,' said Derek angrily.

'With good reason.'

'He's learnt his lesson.'

'Gerry learns no lessons. I just can't get over it, Derek. Gerry's finally blown it and you want to join him.'

'I'll keep him on the straight and narrow.'

'Impossible. He's a cowboy.'

'He needs a chance.'

'Why you?'

'*I* need a chance.'

'We've given you one.'

'I'm a number two here.'

'It's an equal partnership.'

'Sure.'

'What does that mean?'

'It means it's time I went off and tried to be a number one.'

'With him?' Jim laughed contemptuously. 'No chance. Anyway, don't you care that you're leaving us high and dry?'

'You've got the kid.'

'He's going back to school next week. And what does he know about mechanics?'

'You know enough to get by. Teach him, he'll learn.'

Jim leant forward in angry exasperation, furious at such bland insensitivity.

In the kitchen Gwen kept repeating silently, 'Let him go, Jim. Just let him go.' She knew her brother of old. She had always dominated him and now it was time for him to find some independence. If he wanted to join Gerry – let him. Of course it was going to be difficult and his departure could not have come at a worse time. But still she hoped Jim would let him go without trouble.

Jim's anger, however, was increasing. 'That kid can only help us when we're around South London. Are you stupid or something?'

'I'm going out.' Derek stood up. He didn't want trouble. In the kitchen Gwen was suddenly grateful to him.

'Going down the boozer? You won't be doing much of that with Gerry. He won't even give you enough for a half of bitter.'

'He's going into something new.'

'He's done that before.'

'Something that's going to work this time. To make money. Not like the Gallopers.'

'The Gallopers is coming back into its own,' yelled Jim. 'The take was good last night.'

'I saw the take. It was lousy.'

'Get out then.'

'I'm going.' Derek had finally lost his temper. 'But I'd like to say something first.'

'Feel free.'

In the kitchen Gwen clenched her fists.

'You're a mean bastard.'

'Get out,' Jim repeated.

Derek slammed the door with considerable force and stamped down the steps.

Jim buried his face in his hands, his whole body shaking with anger.

'Let him go and good riddance,' Gwen said as she emerged from the kitchen. She put her hands on his rigid shoulders and began to massage them. 'We'll be better off without him.'

But Jim couldn't accept her comfort. 'He's right.'

'What?'

'We're finished.'

'Rubbish.'

'I can't operate with a kid.'

'No?'

He looked up. 'What do you mean?'

'He's a good kid,' she said.

'A kid who's going back to school. A kid who can only work weekends.'

'Is he?' Gwen asked as she opened the door. 'Leroy!' she bellowed. 'Come in here.'

Leroy sat in the seat that Derek had just vacated, looking at Jim nervous anticipation. Had he done something wrong?

But it was Gwen who started the discussion. 'We've

just said goodbye to Derek,' she said. Leroy stared at her. Were they going to say goodbye to him too? 'So we're looking for someone full time.'

'OK. I understand. It's been good fun and . . .' His voice shook as it tailed away in disappointment.

'We've been very impressed with you, son,' said Jim quickly.

'Thanks.'

'So I'm offering you a full-time job. Maybe a partnership when you're older.' Leroy's mouth dropped open. 'It's going to be tough, though. You'll have to learn mechanics from me, and I don't know much about them so you'll have to go to night school. And it'll be really hard work, day in, day out.'

'Do you really mean it?'

'I'm not in the habit of joking about my business,' said Jim rather pompously. 'It's my life, and I'll be even more straight with you and say that the ride isn't taking enough. The public thinks it's tame nowadays. But it's been in the family too long for me to give it up. We love it, see. We don't want a Moon Shot.'

'What do you think, Leroy?' asked Gwen quietly. 'It's a lot to spring on you. We'd be taking a gamble – and so would you. After all you don't come from a travelling background as we do.' She looked at him steadily. 'It's a hell of a big decision all round. And if you've got exams to take at school then we'll think again.'

'No,' said Leroy. 'I'm not the exam type.'

'When would you leave school?'

'I could have left this year. But there's no work and they said I could stay another year, do this new sixth form course and they'd try and find me some work experience.'

'You've got it,' said Jim. 'Plenty of work experience.'

'What about your parents?' asked Gwen.

Leroy shrugged. 'What about them?'

'They've got to give permission. And are you sure *you* really want the job, Leroy? It's a hard life.'

'Do I want it?' he yelled. 'Don't you understand, I'd *love* to do it. And I'll learn and go to night school and . . .'

'We should talk to your parents,' said Jim. 'Can you bring them down here after we close? Or is that too late?'

'No,' said Leroy. 'They're nightbirds anyway.' He leapt to his feet. 'You know what?'

'What?'

'This is the best thing that's ever happened to me.'

'I'm going to join the fair,' Leroy yelled at Gallica as the roundabout whirled noisily around them.

'You're what?'

'It's going to be great. I'll be going all over the country with them.'

'What about your parents?'

'I'll sort them out,' he said grandly.

Gallica almost said what about me? But how could she? She'd only met him yesterday and she hardly knew him at all. A great weight of depression suddenly settled on her. She looked at Leroy's muscular body as he whirled away from her, collecting tickets.

'When can I see you?' she shouted above the music as he came round the next time.

'I don't know.'

He sounded vague. I've gone out of his life already, she thought miserably.

But when he came round again Leroy said, 'How about tomorrow afternoon? I have a break then. Don't know where, though.'

She waited patiently for his next appearance. Then she said with as much authority as she could muster, 'Meet me at the farm at two. You know where that is?'

'Yeah. The Urban Farm. We went there from school. OK. See you then.'

He was gone.

Derek was talking to an exhausted Gerry in his trailer. Gerry had just received a visit from the police. It had been a particularly unpleasant experience.

'What happened?' Derek was anxious. It had been a terrific wrench leaving Jim and Gwen – like losing a family. But he couldn't go on earning peanuts for slave labour, and he reckoned he could go a long way with Gerry with his own mastery of mechanics and Gerry's ideas.

'The ride's got to be inspected. See if I was doing a naughty.'

'What are they going to find?' asked Derek suspiciously.

'That I cut a few maintenance corners. They can't prove a thing.' He sounded very confident.

'Is it going to be so easy to re-open with the same equipment?' Derek still felt uneasy. The large amount of money that Gerry had promised him seemed a long way away.

'We're going to start from scratch,' said Gerry. 'Build something new.' There was a long silence. 'Want something in advance?' he added.

'Yeah.'

'How much? Five hundred do?'

'How come you got so much money?'

'Me old auntie died, didn't she? Left me a few grand.'

'I've heard that one before.' But Derek was grinning. Things were definitely looking up.

'It's true, oddly enough.' There was a trace of sadness in Gerry's voice. He went to a wall safe and took the money out.

'How are you going to make all this money *and* outwit the Guild?' said Derek, stuffing the roll of notes into his pocket with difficulty.

'I'm not *doing* any outwitting,' Gerry protested. 'I'm going to build a new ride. I'm going to call it To Hell And Back – kind of switchback ride.'

'Sounds the same to me.'

'It'll be faster,' said Gerry happily. 'We'll build it down at Chertsey and be back on the road in a month.'

'What about the Guild?'

'They'll pass it. Now I've got a good mechanic I'll get me green ticket back!' Gerry grinned and added abruptly, 'How's Jim going to get on without you?'

'Badly.' Derek felt a sudden and unfamiliar twinge of guilt.

'So that's it, Mum,' said Leroy. She looked horrified, but he had expected that. Leroy was relying on Dad to help him. His new dad.

'Sebastian!' Mum yelled. 'Come and hear this.'

He came shambling in, looking exhausted. Life on the dole was hitting him as hard as Mick Newby.

'What do you want?' He didn't sound in the best of moods.

'Leroy wants to join the fair.'

'I've been offered a job, Dad. Straight up. And Jim and Gwen want to see you. Both of you.'

'You're not going on no fair – ' Mum was working herself up into a fine old rage.

Leroy turned to Dad. Would he be angry? And would they now simply return to their old relationship?

A slow smile began to spread over Sebastian's face. 'Now see here, Edna,' he said. 'We're not going to pass up giving this boy a chance of a job, are we?'

'We are!' she said, still outraged. 'That's no job he's been offered.'

'They want to see you tonight,' said Leroy hopefully. 'They're really nice people and they want to tell you what they're doing for me.'

'Doing you is the word,' muttered Mum darkly.

'If these guys are on the level then I think we should go ahead,' said Sebastian.

'I'd rather he went to college,' Mum began, but Sebastian was ready for her.

'Where did education get me? I didn't do so bad at school and all I got was a bum job as a packer. And I stayed a packer till I got so bored I agreed to wink at that inside job which got me nicked.'

But she was hardly listening. 'And if it all comes to pieces? What does he do then?'

'He'll have had some experience of life, won't he?'

Mum stared at both of them helplessly, then her resistance began to crumble. She wanted to please Dad, Leroy suddenly realised. She wanted so much to make a proper family life for them all. 'I shall have to talk very carefully to these people,' she said. 'I don't want to think of my boy traipsing round the country getting into all kinds of scrapes.' She looked at Sebastian and then at Leroy and smiled at them lovingly. 'Still if it's a job that – '

'Keeps him straight?' Sebastian went across and hugged her plump shoulders. 'Keeps him off the streets. Right!' He turned to Leroy. 'You let anyone down, son, and you really does a dive.' Sebastian walked out of the room.

'Where's he going?' asked Leroy.

'He wants to be on his own.'

'But why?'

'Because your dad's thinking he's made such a mess of his life. And he wants you to be happy, Leroy. Happy and straight.'

Five

Sharon was walking up the old railway track with Imran. He was gloomy and silent and had hardly spoken a word to her since they had met. The afternoon was glorious, with a warm sun beating down on them. There was a mellow brambly smell coming from the bushes and Sharon was blackberrying.

'What's up?'

'You know what's up,' he said.

'You've got to – '

'Make allowances for him. I'm going to smash his silly-looking face in before I go.'

'Go?' Sharon looked up from the blackberry bush. She had been eating some and her mouth was stained purple with the berry juice.

'I'm going to the academy. Next month.'

She stared at him in bewilderment, unable to work out whether he really meant it this time or if it was just one of his threats. But there was something in his face that made her uneasy. Something resolute and yet frightened.

'Imran – ' she began hesitantly, not really knowing what to say.

'I know. I've said it all before. But the ticket came through last night. My uncle brought it. At first I didn't want to go. But I do now. I can see how things were between you and Mick – and how I've come between you.'

'Don't be such an idiot. Any boy would make him jealous.'

'I'm sorry, Sharon.'

'I don't believe you.' But this time she knew he was serious.

Imran felt in his pocket and brought out the air ticket. It looked horribly real.

'I'm better off in Pakistan.'

'No! I love you. I want you.'

'And I love you too.' He drew her to him.

'I'll talk to Mick.'

'It won't do any good.'

Sharon burst into tears. 'I love you,' she said. Suddenly everything had collapsed. She looked up at the bright blue sky and then down at the blackberries in her bowl. It just couldn't be happening. But it was. 'Don't you love *me*?'

'Of course I do.'

'Then – '

'It's for the best, Sharon.' He sounded like an old man. He sounded like a father. 'It really is for the best.'

There was a terrible finality to his words.

Leroy and Gallica were walking down the old track too, although they had paused higher up than Imran and Sharon. They sat on the bank and Gallica wondered how long she would have to wait before he kissed her – or would she have to kiss him? She was almost trembling as she sat there, and prayed that he would not notice how agitated she was. But Leroy seemed distracted, full of his new job on the fair. She listened patiently as he told her all about it, repeating himself several times in his enthusiasm. Her main worry was that she was not going to see him for weeks on end, but this was a little allayed when he told her that many of the venues for the Gallopers were around London.

'What did your parents say?' she asked, wondering how big the row had been. She was almost disappointed when he told her how easily his mum had caved in, faced with his dad's own enthusiasm. He's having it too easy, she thought jealously. It wasn't fair that he was going to get the job without a row and without her being able to offer a shoulder to cry on.

She was beginning to feel more and more redundant when he suddenly turned to her and said, 'I do like you a lot, Gallica.'

He's noticed my existence at last, she thought petulantly. She looked up at the gentle blue of the afternoon sky. It's all too damned perfect, she thought. Suddenly she wanted a thunderstorm to burst over their heads.

Mick had decided to spend the afternoon spying on his sister. He had a terrible hangover and felt exhausted. First of all there had been Gerry's, then last night he'd had a skinful too. Usually he would have welcomed the extra fatigue but throughout a morning in bed he kept surfacing and worrying about what he would be expected to do for the money he had been promised. His sense of isolation increased, and when he heard Sharon on the phone making the arrangement with Imran he determined to follow her. He didn't know what he was going to do when he got there – maybe just watch them, or maybe do something else. Make Imran's life a misery in some sort of way. How he longed to pick a fight with him and flatten him in front of Sharon. He had had that thought ever since he had first known Imran was going out with his sister. And now, with a bit of luck, the opportunity was coming nearer. He wandered along the overgrown embankment, thankful for the overhanging foliage.

'But you won't have time to see me,' pronounced Gallica. That should get him to make a decision. 'Working on a fair is a full-time job,' she added reprovingly, realising that she was sounding parental. But she had not counted on Leroy's optimism.

'I haven't sold myself to Jim North or his family,' he said. 'I shall have my time off all right.'

Suddenly he leant over and kissed her and she was completely taken aback. His lips were warm and loving and there was a strength and purpose behind them that she had entirely underestimated. As he took her in his arms she felt a sudden wild rush of elation. He likes me after all. Suddenly, to her intense horror, she realised that she had spoken the words aloud. He would think she was a right idiot.

But all he said was, 'You bet I like you. And I'm going to prove it.' She felt the weight of his body on top of her.

It was Gallica who saw Mick first.

'There's someone there.'

Leroy sat up. 'What's up with you?'

'I told you – I saw someone move.'

He looked at the overgrown embankment. 'Don't spoil it now.'

'I'm not.' It was the last thing she wanted to do. But if there was someone watching . . .

Leroy groaned. 'I'll go and see.'

Walking up the embankment was difficult. There were a lot of brambles and he had to push his way through. 'There's no one here,' he said as he stood up on the skyline.

He looks wonderful there, thought Gallica. Now she wanted him more than ever. 'Come back then.'

'Were you enjoying that?' He sat down on top of the embankment. The sun was behind him, picking out his tight curls in a gold light.

'You know I was.'

'Come and get me then.'

Gallica began to climb the bank.

Mick edged his way out of a thorn bush and walked stealthily on. A few minutes later he could see them.

They were sitting talking. Arguing maybe, he thought hopefully. Slowly, he inched his way down towards them – and then broke cover.

'What the hell do you want?' Sharon was the first to see him.

Imran stood up and she grabbed at his hand. He brushed it away. The humour of it suddenly struck him. It was like an old western. The tall dark stranger was in town, waiting for his enemy to arrive. Mick the kid. Imran wanted to laugh but couldn't, knowing that what he had been trying to avoid for so long had irrevocably arrived. There was no way out now. He would have to fight.

'Settle an old score.'

It was incredible, thought Imran. Mick seemed to be talking like a cowboy. Were they sharing the same fantasy?

'Go to hell,' said Sharon.

'That's not a nice greeting, little sister.'

'Don't come here and cause trouble.'

'This is between him and me,' said Mick, looking down at Imran. 'We'll settle it now – unless you want to chicken out.'

Sharon screamed, just as Gallica and Leroy were rolling down the embankment together.

'What the hell?' asked Leroy as he pushed her off him at the bottom. 'It's like Piccadilly Circus up here.'

Sharon screamed again and then began to call for help.

'Who is it?' Leroy was standing there, confused, but Gallica knew exactly who it was.

'Sharon. She's in trouble.' She struggled to her feet, brushing herself down, and began to run along the narrow overgrown path.

Mick and Imran were circling each other when they arrived and Sharon was making little darting rushes at her brother, who kept savagely pushing her away.

Blimey, thought Leroy, this looks really bad.

'Stop him,' whispered Sharon. 'You must stop him.'

'Stop that now,' Leroy snapped dutifully and advanced a couple of paces. We could take him, he thought. It's three against one. He looked at Sharon. She obviously wasn't going to be much use. Half-crouched, shaking, her cheeks were streaked with tears.

Mick pulled something out of his pocket. It shone in the late afternoon sun.

'Put it down,' said Imran. 'I'll fight you, but without a knife.'

'This is to warn you two off,' Mick sneered. 'Get going, this is a private quarrel.'

'No,' said Gallica as she began to walk towards him. 'I'm not going anywhere.'

Leroy moved forward but she was ahead of him, walking purposefully, her hand outstretched. Now she was within touching distance.

'Give it to me.'

'Get away.' There was a faint note of unease in

Mick's voice and Gallica took full advantage of it. She grasped his wrist and held on hard.

'Take your hand away.'

'No.'

'I'll stick you.'

'Go ahead.'

Leroy and Imran were moving in now and it was only Sharon who was a terrified spectator. Suddenly Mick wrenched his hand away and the knife missed Gallica's fingers by a whisker. He backed off and then ran up the embankment. He stood there, locking his eyes to Imran's.

'I'll be back,' he said and then turned and ran.

Gallica put her arms round Sharon, comforting her as she wept. Leroy turned to Imran.

'What got into him?'

'He hates my guts.'

'Yeah, he must do. Somebody should do something about that guy – he's lethal.'

'He'll be back,' said Imran quietly. 'You heard him say it.'

Leroy didn't know what to say. He turned to Gallica. 'You were fantastic,' he said touching her hand lightly. 'Absolutely fantastic.'

Gallica shook her head and helped her friend to sit down on the grass. Sharon was still shaking.

'Who is he?' asked Leroy. 'Who was that crazy guy?'

'My brother,' said Sharon and the tears poured down her cheeks like twin rivers.

Six

Each night Leroy had returned home exhausted from the fair. But he knew he was doing well and the conversation that his parents had had with Jim and Gwen seemed to have satisfied them. Even his mother had been convinced of their honesty and integrity.

'We'll always pay him a fair wage and we're going to send him to night school straightaway,' Gwen had said. His father had been delighted and his mother cautiously reassured.

Now, on the last night of the fair, as Leroy drifted off to sleep he had never felt so tired – and so contented. He had told his gran all about it and although he didn't think she really understood what he was talking about, he knew she was pleased that he had a job and was enjoying it. Leroy dreamt of her that night. She was riding the Gallopers with a bottle of her favourite stout in her hand.

'This is the life,' she yelled.

He woke up laughing.

Jim and Gwen spent most of their free time counting money and worrying. The take was still well down;

while the other rides did well, Gallopers often revolved with less than half its capacity of riders.

'He's a good lad,' said Jim. 'But his work with us may be shorter than he thinks.'

Gallica and Sharon met at break in the Starling Comprehensive playground for the first time since Mick's attack. They stood in the shelter of the concrete arches that were mock cloisters to the tar-macadam playing area. The school was enormous and had only been open for two years. It was very different from its run-down predecessor, and although the buildings had been knocked about a bit and there was a liberal display of graffiti everywhere, the rooms were light and airy and there was an air of hope.

'I'll never thank you enough for what you did the other day,' said Sharon.

It was drizzling with rain and the playground was covered in a fine sheet of water. The buildings were reflected in it; distorted shapes on a windswept black lake.

'I hope Leroy was proud of you,' she added.

'I was terrified,' said Gallica. 'What can it be like living with Mick?'

'He lives in bed. He only comes out in the afternoons.'

'What made him attack Imran like that?'

'He's jealous of Imran. We used to be really close.' Sharon paused. 'I do understand what he feels,' she added sadly. 'Anyway he doesn't have to worry any more,' her voice broke.

'Why?'

'Imran's going to Pakistain, to the Military Academy. I never thought he'd go. I thought it was just a dream. But now he's had a flight booked and he's going next month.'

'Oh no.' Gallica looked really upset. She thought about it for a bit. 'Have you told Mick?' she asked.

'No.'

'Wouldn't it be better?'

'I just can't bring myself to speak to him.'

'Shall I?'

Sharon hesitated. 'Would you?'

'It'd be safer for Imran if I did. I mean, Mick could have a go at him anytime, couldn't he?'

'I'll tell him,' said Sharon. 'You can't – not after what you did.'

'Tell him tonight.' Gallica was insistent.

'I promise.' There was a long silence as they watched the rain begin to increase, pitting the water on the playground until it was churned into miniature waves. 'What about Leroy then?'

'I really fancy him,' replied Gallica. 'I think about him all the time.'

'I'm so glad.' Sharon squeezed her hand.

'I don't see much of him. That wretched merry-go-round. He's obsessed with it. And they're going to travel.'

'Not as far as Pakistan,' sighed Sharon.

* * *

'We could have to sell up.' Jim sat on the steps of the caravan the next morning while the twins played with toy cars on the concrete. Gwen put down her newspaper. She found she was trembling inside.

'The take doesn't give us a living, not even for just the two of us,' continued Jim. 'Looks like Derek got out at the right time.'

'I've got an idea – if you want to hear it.'

'What idea?'

'We've always gone round the fairs. Why can't we think of somewhere else?'

'Southend Pier?'

'Covent Garden.'

He stared at her as if she had gone mad.

'The South Bank or one of them big parks.'

'You gone barmy?'

'No, I'm being practical. Showing a bit of commonsense. We're a tradition, we're nostalgia. Now, no one wants to ride if we're right next door to that Moon Shot. But suppose we were on our own?'

'A museum piece?'

'One that's fun. Takes people back a bit.'

Jim gave a grudging smile. 'Now that's not a bad idea.' Then the smile disappeared. 'But how do we get the work?'

'Remember Angus?'

'Big-hearted Angus? The Showmans' Showman. What a berk. He was the one who got us in that park in Skegness. The park no one went to.'

'He's an agent.'

'He's a cowboy.'

'And he's got contacts.'

'Look, Gwen – '

'I'm going to see him.'

'When?'

'Now.'

She gathered herself up and shouted at the twins, 'You're going to help your dad and Leroy for the day.'

They scampered up, half their breakfast still round their mouths and their arms and legs filthy.

'I want you two cleaned up,' Gwen declared and when they began to moan, she yelled, 'Shut up, both of you. You've got to pull your weight.'

'Mick.'

'I'm in bed.'

'I want to talk.'

'And I don't want to talk to you.'

Nevertheless she pushed her way into his bedroom. It was eleven o'clock and both her parents were out at work. Sharon had chosen her time carefully, taking a morning off school to trap Mick at his most vulnerable. He seemed to disappear somewhere mysterious in the afternoons and she wanted to make sure of catching him.

Mrs Newby had given up cleaning Mick's bedroom months ago and now it was no more than a filthy, stuffy tip with the curtains firmly closed and mounds of clothes and dirty cups and plates lying all over the floor. Sharon picked her way over them and arrived at her brother's bedside. He was not a pleasant sight, unshaved and frowsty in the grey light.

'Mick.'

'I'm asleep.'

She was instantly reminded of him as a child, turning away from his angry father who had discovered he had lifted money from his mother's purse. 'I'm asleep,' he had said as he rolled away from the gym shoe that her father had been wielding. But he had been beaten all the same.

'I want to talk.'

'Nothing to talk about.'

'I think there is. Imran's going to Pakistan. To the Military Academy.'

'Is he, my arse.'

'I promise you, he is. He's going next month. It's all settled and he's got his air ticket.'

Mick rolled over and sat up. He still looked a little boy, but this time a little boy who had just been offered a treat.

'You straight up?'

'Yes.'

'He's actually going? And you and me are going to be together again?'

'I don't want him to go, Mick. Don't be such a bloody kid.'

'I'm not a kid. I'm just glad he's going. And so will Dad and Mum be.'

'Stick to your own kind,' she said bitterly.

'Well, why not?'

'You wouldn't like anyone I went with.'

'If he was a white guy we'd be mates.'
'Why can't you be mates with Imran?'
'Because he's not one of us. Got funny ways, them lot, and they treat their women bad. You'd be a slave to him. You seen them Muslim women?'
'Shut up.'
'We could be mates again.'
'Maybe.' She was trying to keep back the tears. 'But if we are to be mates you got to do something for me.'
'What?' He sounded suspicious.
'Never let yourself have a go like that again.'
He said nothing.
'Because if you do I promise I'll never speak to you again.'
'I hate the bastard.'
'He's going away.' Her voice broke but Mick didn't seem to notice.
'All right.'
'You promise?'
'I promise.'
'Thanks, Mick.'
She backed away as he turned over contentedly. Quite soon he began to snore.

Later that night, after she had come back from school, Sharon confronted her parents over the supper table. There was never very much conversation over the Newby table; indeed her father rarely spoke at all, hiding himself for the most part behind a newspaper.

But Sharon's opening comment made him put his newspaper down pretty fast.

'Imran's going back to Pakistan.'

There was a long silence during which she saw her parents exchanging glances. It made her temper rise to think of those glances. How could they be so narrow? They didn't even know Imran, so what right did they have to reject him? They didn't know anything about what Mick had done either and she didn't propose to tell them.

'Well, my dear,' her father began, and before she could stop herself Sharon brought out a very good imitation of his voice and manner:

'Perhaps it's a good thing.'

'What has got into you?' asked her mother angrily. 'You're not the girl you used to be.'

'I *do* think it's a good thing,' said her father. 'A very good thing. Now perhaps you'll come down to earth and get back to your studies.'

Sharon rose to her feet. 'For your information, I never left my studies. But now I'll probably give it all up. Nothing means anything to me any more. Not now he's going.' Her rage spilled out and she ran up to her father, tearing the newspaper out of his hand and screaming, 'I love him. Don't you understand that word? Don't you understand that word at all?'

And with that she ran out of the room and straight out of the front door. It was raining and she didn't know where she was going. She didn't even care.

* * *

'Sharon.'

Sharon looked up as she hurried past the supermarket and saw Imran's father, Mr Dapor. He was a small man with a gentle, self-effacing manner. He looked friendly but she had rarely spoken to him. She had never been inside Imran's home. They had been two nomads, always searching for somewhere to be together. And mainly that somewhere had been the tatty confines of the youth club.

'Yes?' She didn't want to speak to anyone; she put her head down, trying to hurry on. But he was determined and stood in her path.

'I would like to speak with you.'

'I'm in a bit of a hurry.'

'It won't take long.'

She allowed herself to be led into the semi-lit supermarket which had been closed for the night.

'Sit down, please.'

She sat at one of the check-out tills while he sat at the other. There was nowhere else to sit and he did not seem to think there was anything ludicrous about it.

'I am sorry.'

'Sorry?' Sharon wondered why she was making it all so difficult for him. He was a kind man and she knew how much Imran loved him.

'That he has to go away. It is his own choice, you know. There has been no parental pressure. He has had the offer to go to the Military Academy from his uncle for some months. And now he has finally decided to take it up.'

'Because of Mick.'

'Your brother? That was a nasty episode, but I do not think so. He wants a change of scene. He has wanted it for some time.'

'I love him,' said Sharon bleakly.

'I am not going to say that you just think you do. I am not going to patronise you.'

She looked across at him in surprise; she had been sure that he was going to.

'What am I going to do?' she asked pathetically. 'What am I going to do?' Sharon began to cry and Mr Dapor got up from his till and came and stood beside her. She knew that he wanted to put his arms round her but did not know how to.

'It is very difficult,' he said inadequately.

'Your family wouldn't have wanted me anyway,' she said.

'That is not true.'

Again she looked at him in surprise.

'We are not bigots. Yes, it is true that I am a religious man and that it would have been easier for me and my wife to have accepted a Muslim girl. Of course it would, but life does not work out that way. We knew that when we first came here from Pakistan. When he comes back, if your love is as strong as it is now, you must marry.'

Sharon stared at him. This was not what she had expected to hear at all. And what was all this talk of marriage? He was going to be away for three years. It was a lifetime. By the time he came back . . .

'I know you are thinking that three years is a long time.'

'It is.'

'Can't you wait?'

'I don't know.'

'Have you talked about it?'

'We've quarrelled about it.'

Mr Dapor smiled.

'Why does he want to go? If it's not because of Mick?'

'Because he does not know his identity.'

'What do you mean?'

He spread his arms and Sharon suddenly felt terribly stupid.

'You must realise that we came here when Imran was four and Naveed had not even been born. Imran and Naveed have been brought up in the West. All that is left of their Pakistan upbringing lies within the walls of our flat and the mosque. And Imran is not a religious boy; even more than Naveed he has become a Western boy. He has Western values and outlook and yet he comes from the East. Do you not see how difficult this is? That is why he is going to Pakistan.'

'To the Military Academy? For three years?'

'If he can't make the grade at the academy he could be back in three weeks.'

'But couldn't he go to Pakistan and not go to the academy? Why does he have to go to be a soldier? He may never come back.'

'He could still change his mind.'

'*What?*'

'He may still change his mind and not want to go.'

'Don't *you* want him to go?'

'We are undecided. It is very difficult for us. We, too, shall miss him very much.'

Sharon now felt totally confused. 'What are you trying to tell me? He is *certain* that he wants to go. I mean – he's got his air ticket.'

Mr Dapor smiled. 'Don't worry. I can still get rid of that.'

'Are you asking me to talk him out of going? Because if you are I don't think I'm going to succeed. His mind is made up.'

'Yes. He is a very stubborn boy. He takes after me, for I can be a very stubborn man.'

'What am I to do?' Sharon stared at Mr Dapor blankly. She felt completely helpless.

'We are very happy at Starling Point. My business has flourished. Do you know that I came here with nothing? I began in a tiny lock-up down the road, but since we have moved on to the estate we have been made very welcome. There is nothing racist about Starling Point. There are no attacks on Asians like there are in other parts of London. Nothing like that at all. Of course, there will always be a few dissenters like your brother. But he is a very unhappy young man because he has no work and no hope of getting work. So, I will make you a deal.'

'A deal?' Sharon was stunned. How could she be having this conversation with Mr Dapor?

'You talk my boy out of going to Pakistan and it will please his mother and me a very great deal. And whether you succeed or not, for I know you will try, I will offer your brother Mick a job here, just as the fairground man has offered a job to the young West Indian boy . . . Oh yes, news travels fast in Starling Point. But I am afraid you will have to do a lot of persuading for he will not want to work for the Pakis. But if he did, the job would be good. I have need of help and the business is still expanding.'

'But I thought you would only want to take on a Pakistani.'

'Naveed is still at school. He can only help at weekends.'

'But . . .'

'You thought I would only take on my own people. I tell you, I am not a bigot. Now, what do you think of my deal?'

'I think it's fantastic.'

'But do you think it would work?'

She shook her head. 'Don't know. Talk Imran out of going to Pakistan and Mick into working for you? I'm not a miracle worker.'

'But that's what we need, of course,' he said. 'And I shall be praying for you.'

Sharon left the supermarket stunned and bewildered. Why had she expected Mr Dapor to be so foreign, so different? She had imagined his religious life would have completely excluded her as a friend of Imran's, let alone a wife. And being his wife took a bit of thinking about; she hadn't even begun to imagine a future and she wasn't sure that she wanted to.

Gradually a new idea lodged in her mind. Mr Dapor might be a Muslim and might come from a faraway country that was almost mythical to her, but he was now part of Starling Point. They all were, whatever their background. But it was Mr Dapor who was showing the way.

Seven

It was three o'clock when Gwen returned. Jim watched her walking across the piazza quite slowly and he knew at once that she had failed. It was a crazy idea anyway, he thought, and they should never have raised their hopes in such a stupid way. He blamed himself for encouraging her. Well, she would need looking after and he yelled at one of the twins to put the kettle on.

Gwen climbed the steps to the trailer slowly and sank down on the sofa, wearily kicking off her shoes.

'Cup of tea?'

'I'm dying for one.'

'Walk far?'

'Bloody miles.'

'Never mind, love. It was worth a try. Anything's worth a try.'

She smiled up at him and, for a blessed moment, Jim thought there would be no need for a painful conversation about a vain quest. Then Dan ruined it by coming straight to the point.

'Are we going to London, Mum?'

She grinned at him and then said, 'Yes.'

Jim stared at her in amazement. 'What?'

'We're going to London, my lovies.' There was a stunned silence then she suddenly shouted, 'Where's that bottle of gin? We're going to celebrate!'

'You must be crazy.' Nasla Dapor poured tea into her husband's cup. It was their special time, four in the afternoon, when they left the supermarket to the staff and came home for the ritual of afternoon tea. They would talk and plan and argue, for although Nasla had been an ordinary Islamic wife in Pakistan, sharing the work-load of the supermarket had made her far more of an equal partner, except when they entertained or the Imam came. Then she reverted to modesty and servitude, with eyes lowered, her tasks domestic. She and her husband Shamra had built the business up together; she with her developing book-keeping skills, he with his grand ideas. But it was Shamra's vision that had seen them through, from lock-up shop to the vast space of the Starling Point supermarket. And she had followed his vision, trying to make the account books flexible enough to accommodate his plans and to afford his mistakes. Nasla loved and trusted her husband for many reasons, not least because he had the courage to turn dreams into reality. But this time she was sure he had gone too far.

'The Newby boy is trouble,' she pronounced.

'Do you remember what it was like when *we* had no money?'

Nasla detected the stubborn note in his voice. This

could be the hardest battle of all. But she knew too much about Mick Newby to be merciful to him.

'You'll do neither him nor us any good,' she said firmly.

'I should give him a chance. *We* got chances.'

'We were not like him.'

'He is Sharon's brother.'

'This friendship has caused problems enough. We don't want any more.'

Nasla felt her husband looking at her in a familiar way. Her heart sank. The look said that he had made his mind – and no one would be able to change it.

'I feel you could regret this,' she said, knowing he would not listen to her but glad she was able to express her opinion.

Leroy had been given the afternoon off so he decided to go fishing down the canal. He wanted to think. So much had happened in his life recently that he had had no time to think at all. And so he set off with his rod and tackle and walked down to the narrow strip of water round the back of Starling Point.

It was a warm, mellow aftrenoon and he could smell the scent of the blackberries that grew thickly in the brambles by the water. He looked down into the dark, sluggishly flowing creek and saw the faces of Gallica and Jim and Gwen. What would he do when the Gallopers moved on? It wasn't going to be so easy. Gallica would be at school and he would be somewhere the other side of London, or even the other side of the country if Jim's fortunes suddenly looked up. Already he was beginning to miss her when she was not there; the incident with Mick had only served to heighten the attraction he felt for her. Then he saw another face in the water and he stared, for the face was real this time.

'Mind if I join you?'

'Sure.'

'Not having a private think?'

'I was, but it's over now. Let's talk.'

'We haven't talked since you were a kid.'

'You weren't here, Dad. It's not your fault.'

'It was my fault I wasn't here,' he said, then added quickly, 'I'm taking over as the club football coach. The under-twelves. Winston's lot.'

'Great.'

'Gives me something to do on a Saturday morning. That only leaves another six and a half days to fill in.'

'Something will turn up, Dad.'

'Will it?' He sighed and lit a cigarette. 'I'm forty-seven and got no bloody chance, son. I'm wasted.'

'No.'

'I've tried for everything there was going. And there's plenty of us in the same boat. Look at young Mick, for instance.'

'What are you saying, Dad?' Sudden alarm bells were ringing in Leroy's mind. 'Mick's rubbish. Vicious, too.'

'Is he? He's only a kid down on his luck. I've been talking to him.'

'Yeah?' Suddenly an awful thought seized Leroy.

Supposing Dad was planning to do something with Mick. Something illegal. 'Dad?'

'Yeah?'

But he could not bring himself to go on, because he knew it would break their new friendship and he couldn't bear that to happen.

'How did you get it then?'

'Walked into the office and asked for it.'

'Couldn't have been as easy as that.'

'Well, it was. Mark you, I got there at the right time.'

Jim leant over and kissed her. 'Miracle worker, you are.'

'I was lucky.'

'Either way, what's the deal?'

'The deal is the Covent Garden precinct. They want a traditional ride up there from the beginning of December right through until the New Year. And, subject to them coming and looking at us, I know we're well in.'

Immediately Jim was nervous. 'They got to inspect us?'

'Not inspect. Just take a look.'

'Supposing he doesn't like it?'

'Gallopers is a good ride, Jim. A wonderful, bloody marvellous, traditional ride in very good nick. And if you don't know that, I do.'

'Dad.'

'Yes?'

'I've got an idea.'

'What's that?' Leroy knew that his father was looking at him very carefully and wondered if he was reading his thoughts, but he ploughed on nevertheless.

'Suppose Jim could make room for a guy on the fair. Someone who was strong, much stronger than me.'

'What are you getting at, son?'

'If I gave up working the Gallopers, Jim would take you on. He'd prefer to. You're stronger than me and you know more than me.'

'But it's your job, son. The one Mum and I are backing so much.'

'Yeah. Maybe it's too risky.'

Sebastian looked at his son very shrewdly. 'Leroy, I don't believe my ears.'

Leroy felt terrible pains in his chest and wondered if his heart was going to break. He could feel the tears stinging at the back of his eyes. If he left the Gallopers his whole world would end. But his world would also end if his dad got into trouble again and had to go back inside.

Sebastian put a hand on his arm. 'What are you trying to tell me, son?' he asked gently.

'Nothing.'

'I think you are.'

'I said nothing, Dad. It's an offer, that's all.'

'You're not thinking you made a mistake about Gallopers?'

'Maybe I am.' Leroy was desperate now. 'Maybe it's too much for me.'

'And maybe not.' Sebastian's hand increased in pressure. 'Do you trust me, Leroy?'

'Course I trust you.'

'Then you get on with your life and I'll get on with mine. I trust you to do that and you should trust me. However difficult the past has been.' He got up. 'You stay fishing and thinking, son. You got a good job there and you're working for good people. I'll find something soon, you see.'

He strode off and Leroy watched him go: a tall, solitary, suddenly very vulnerable figure against the twin towers of Starling Point.

Leroy was first to hear the good news when he turned up at work. He was still feeling worried, but the news that they were going to work in Covent Garden, of all places, over Christmas made him wildly excited, glossing over his doubts of the afternoon. Gallica would easily be able to take the train and come and see him, and maybe even stay if he could persuade Jim and Gwen. And as for Dad, well maybe he had just been looking on the worst side.

'We're going to have to work like hell on the ride,' said Jim, bringing him sharply back to reality. Leroy looked at the gleaming paint and harnesses and wondered how they could work harder. But then he realised that Jim was nervous and that, yes, he would work himself into the ground for him.

'I could work extra hours, Jim,' Leroy volunteered but Gwen intervened.

'You work hard enough already, son.' She put her hand on Leroy's shoulder. 'You're proving yourself one of us – a real showman.'

Leroy let out such a whoop of joy that even Jim, stage fright and all, had to grin.

A Wimpy Bar was not the best place to have a dramatic confrontation, but it was Sharon's first chance to have a private discussion with Imran about Pakistan. Time was slipping by and she was getting desperate. Somehow she had lured him into the steamy chrome bar and, over a coffee, a doughnut and a sad-looking cheeseburger, she was prepared to fight to the death. But Imran had gone curiously wooden, and his old carefree rebellious self was absent. It was as if he had built a wall round himself.

'I want to talk,' she said, biting deep into her doughnut and then realising she couldn't because her mouth was so full. She felt a fool as she made idiotic noises and the chewed bits of doughnut stuck to her gullet. Suddenly she panicked. Would she ever get this doughnut out of her mouth? Would she ever be able to speak again? But despite her obvious problem Imran did not smile at all. He looked lost in himself as if the real Imran had already gone to Pakistan.

Eventually she managed to swallow the doughnut and, taking a huge swig of coffee, she repeated herself again.

'I want to talk.'

'What about?' His voice was expressionless.

'Don't go. Please. We can work things out.'

'It's all fixed.' His voice was weary and distant. He looked down at his cheeseburger with a kind of disdain. And he used to love them, she thought, remembering times he had eaten two.

'Imran, I want to ask you something.'

'Yes?' he said patiently.

'If you go, you won't come back.'

'I don't know. It's a long training.'

'Yes, that's what I mean. Look, I know we're young . . .'

He suddenly looked her straight in the eye and she wondered if he knew what she was going to say.

'Why don't we go away somewhere and live together? Somewhere far away from Starling Point?'

He smiled and shook his head. 'Your parents . . .'

'To hell with them.'

'And my military career.' He sounded absurdly pompous and she could have hit him.

'Do you love me?'

Suddenly the old Imran returned, if only fleetingly. 'You know I do.'

'Then why are you going away?' Her voice broke.

'You know why. I've told you a dozen times. I am not acceptable to your family.'

'Do you realise that your dad is going to offer Mick a job in the supermarket?'

Instead of looking angry Imran merely laughed. 'My father always was a crazy idealist. Ever since he's come here, he's had a love affair with this country. Mick wouldn't take the job and your parents wouldn't let him.'

Sharon was silent, her thoughts racing desperately. Every moment they sat here she was losing him; she could literally feel him withdrawing from her.

'We could go to Hastings. It's cheap down there.'

He shook his head. 'There'd be too much trouble.'

'Don't you want to?' she asked angrily, and a middle-aged couple looked up from their meal. They were both in raincoats, both silent, and all too attentive to other people's conversations. She could have screamed. She and Imran had so much to live for and so much to share together.

For another brief instant Imran seemed his old self. 'If it was possible, I'd really want to,' he said and the simple little speech moved her to tears. At her obvious misery he temporised. 'We could go for a day,' he said. 'Why don't we do that?'

And because it was the only shred she had to hang on to, Sharon tearfully agreed.

'Lovers' tiff,' whispered the female part of the middle-aged couple to the male.

'They get younger every day,' he replied. 'It's not right.'

Sharon glanced at them, knowing what they were saying by instinct. She suddenly remembered part of a poem that one of her teachers had read out to them in class. Who was it by? Stevie someone or other. Smith was it?

'Children who paddle where the ocean bed shelves
steeply

Must take great care they do not,
Paddle too deeply.'

Thus spake the awful ageing couple
Whose heart the years had turned to rubble.

But the little children, to save any bother,
Let it in at one ear and out at the other.

She was surprised that she had remembered the whole poem, but as she looked at the middle-aged couple and then back at Imran she suddenly knew what it meant.

Eight

Leroy was exhausted by the time he had finished at the fair that night, but he was still very excited by the prospect of going to Covent Garden and, more important than that, at how much the Norths valued him. He had never really felt valued in his life, and now he knew what it felt like. It was fantastic. He had promised to return early the next day so that he could begin work with Jim on every bit of the ride, polishing and painting, restoring every tiny blemish. Now he was hungry and suddenly fancied the idea of some fish and chips.

Yawning, Leroy hurried down the streets outside Starling Point to the alley by the railway track where the chippy was. He looked at his watch. It was nearly midnight. Then he paused. Ahead of him were two familiar figures talking and walking slowly, sharing chips from a bag. Suddenly Leroy didn't feel hungry any more. The two figures in front of him were Mick and his dad. And they were talking earnestly.

Next morning Gerry and Derek towed away their ride to a field in Surrey which many of the showmen rented to repair their machinery during the winter months. Jim watched them roll past, the battered old truck looking barely roadworthy.

'Good luck to 'em,' said Gwen, while one of the twins howled in the background. 'We're going places, they're going nowhere.'

In the cab of the van Gerry was saying very much the opposite.

'Once we get this fixed up we're going to be in the money.'

'Yeah,' said Derek. 'So you say.'

Word had already gone round that the Gallopers had been booked for Covent Garden and Derek felt sick. He had definitely made a mistake but he knew there was no way of going back. Firstly his pride wouldn't let him, and secondly the black kid seemed to have won their hearts. He felt jealous and regretful at the same time. What he could have seen in Gerry was beyond him now. The guy was totally disorganised and, what was worse, he was a lousy mechanic. Derek determined he would take the money and run, particularly as Gerry had plans to build a wall of death in a chain of cars running round a steel drum. He knew the idea would never get past the Guild, not after all that had happened.

Living with Gerry was another hazard. He kept the trailer like a tip and spent most of his time at the pub. Although he only had the haziest idea of his background, Derek had the strong feeling that Gerry was trying to prove himself so hard that he had practically lost all touch with reality. He seemed to be perpetually racing to keep up with his ambitions – and never quite reaching them. Also, he seemed to expect Derek to be some kind of domestic skivvy, which did not suit him in the least, particularly when he was used to being so well looked after by his sister. We're a right pair, thought Derek. But we're not going to be a pair much longer. Directly I get my next payment I'll be off. Fast.

'And don't you worry about them Norths.' Gerry's voice broke in on his thoughts.

'No?'

'Them Norths are going to get their come-uppance all right. They won't be reporting me to the Guild again.'

There was so much hatred in Gerry's voice that Derek knew he had gone beyond his usual display of bravado. Vaguely he wondered what he had in mind, but he dismissed whatever he was planning as a non-event; Gerry would never manage to organise himself sufficiently to carry it out.

For years now, Derek had relied on his sister to boost him up. Gwen had always been more energetic, more purposeful than him. Home life hadn't been much. There had only been Mum and she, like him, was weak. She had met a man who ran a Ghost Train and they travelled the country with it, never making much money. They were always in the pubs and clubs at night and it had been Gwen who had brought him up. He still saw her more as a mother than a sister and he had been dependent on her for so long. Now he had messed up his first stab at going it alone.

There was no going back to Gwen now, however many times he yearned to.

All he could do was to try and persuade Gerry to give him some more of the promised money and then he would try somewhere else. Surely there must be a successful showman who needed a good mechanic?

The memory of one of Gwen's fry-ups slipped into Derek's mind. He could almost smell the onions. Life was cruel, he thought, as Gerry turned up the radio to an unbearable pitch.

'Mick.'

'What the hell do you want?'

'A talk.'

'If it's about your nig-nog boyfriend again . . .'

Sharon had found her brother stretched out on the sofa in the living room and seized her chance before he switched on the telly. Tomorrow there was a school closure for staff training, and she and Imran were going to spend this precious day in Hastings, so she was still in with a chance, albeit a slim one, and it gave her a faint kind of optimism. She knew she would need it to put the proposition to Mick, and she realised that in a few seconds he would be laughing in her face. But she had liked Mr Dapor so much that she was determined to give his offer a chance whether his son thought he was a crazy idealist or not. Perhaps the world should be full of crazy idealists, she thought. Then it would be a better place.

'It's not about Imran. It's about a job.'

'What job? I'm not going back to that slaughterhouse.'

'No one's asking you to. I'm talking about a job in a supermarket. With good prospects.'

For a moment he stared at her and she was shocked by the sudden hope in his eyes. Then they clouded with suspicion.

'What you on about?'

'I'm on about a job.'

'Where is it?'

She took a deep breath but still hedged. 'In a supermarket.'

'You told me that.'

'In a local one. The one that belongs to the Dapors.'

'You're joking.'

'No. Mr Dapor *wants* you to do it. He could offer you . . .'

'I see.' Mick laughed bitterly. 'I see what you're all up to. If I become his man then it will go easier for you and the nig-nog.'

'No. It's a genuine offer. Imran is still dead set on going to Pakistan.'

'There's something in this.'

'There's nothing in this.'

'I wouldn't be seen dead working for them Pakis.'

'Please yourself.'

She'd expected him to say all this, but even so there was a leaden feeling in her chest that threatened to bear her right down.

'It's a good offer,' she said. 'You ought to think it over.'

'I told you. No way.'

She turned away. 'You're a fool.'

'And you're trying it on.'

'You don't know a good offer when you see one.'

'That's no offer. But I've had another and I'm taking it up.'

'What is it?'

'None of your business. But it's a good one and I'm going to be in the loot.'

'Is it on the level?'

'I told you – mind your own business.'

Sharon walked out and slammed the door.

Sharon and Imran took the earliest train they could to Hastings, and at nine on a glorious late September morning they were in a little café in a deserted car park on the front. They had bacon and eggs, fried bread, fried potatoes, sausages, tomatoes, hot sweet tea with condensed milk and loads of bread and butter. There was no one else in the café and the proprietor, a very small man with a pasty face and hard eyes, was immersed in a copy of *The Sun*. The windows of the little café were steamed up and they sat there silently, the little man rustling his newspaper and the kettle gently whispering on the range. Then the door was thrust open and a rush of cold, sea-scented wind blew through the café. Sharon looked at Imran hopelessly. Could she ever manage to make him change his mind?

Minutes later, they were walking over the flat dry sand that the receding tide had left behind. A few gulls called and there was the rattle of a milkfloat, but apart from that there was complete silence on the beach. It was as if they were in their own unique world – a world that no one could possibly interfere with.

They made their way round the base of the cliffs at Fairlight, and then climbed up into the walkway that ran through trees and scrub.

'We came here for a holiday once,' said Imran suddenly. 'I found a little cave and always wanted to spend the night in it. I'm sure it'd be quite warm. It's phosphorous at night. It glows all the way along the underneath of the cliff.'

They walked on and eventually found the cave that was a couple of metres above the shoreline. It was clean and warm and smelt of the sea, although it was clear that the tide did not reach it.

Sharon was beginning to feel the joy of living for the moment: of time suspended. She no longer sought to persuade him. They were together and that was all that mattered.

The sea sighed far out below them and a gull glided over the rock pools, diving down sporadically in search of food. The sun was climbing in the sky, a rather pale watery sun but its warmth struck their faces; then it was gone behind a cloud, leaving a freshness that seemed like the beginning of a new world.

'Let's go back to the beach,' he said.

Walking across the beach and among the tide-stranded pools was a marvellous experience and they both felt so happy that they began to run over the slippery rocks. They leapt and jumped as if they were young children, and although they often held hands they never slipped at all. A light wind was blowing at the edge of the sea and they sat down on a seaweed-strewn rock and took off their shoes and socks and bathed their feet. It was delightfully cool and the silver water ran between their toes with an incredible softness.

They sat and watched the horizon. A fishing boat chugged across the bay and a man waved at them from the deck. They waved back. They were castaways on an island, thought Imran. They would live in the cave forever and fish by day. There would be berries and later they would build a house of driftwood. He kissed Sharon on her warm sweet lips and they fell back against the rock, their bodies intertwined.

Later they ate a picnic on the beach and even the shop-bought sandwiches tasted magnificent. A few people walked past, mainly with dogs, but they ignored Imran and Sharon so that they still felt totally alone. The sea splashed gently up over the rocks and the heat of the sun intensified. Imran took off his shirt and again they lay in each other's arms, Sharon nuzzling her face into his brown, firm, sea-smelling flesh.

'Do you want to go into the town?' he asked. They had spent the whole day on the beach but the evening was closing in now, and a little chilling wind had sprung up and was ruffling the surface of the incoming tide.

'No,' said Sharon. 'Let's go back to that cave.'

It was dry but not very warm in there and Imran suggested making a fire. 'I brought some matches,' he said.

He gathered some driftwood and after five minutes the wood caught and began to blaze up, crackling and emitting a strong briny smell.

'You haven't asked me,' he said suddenly.

'No.'

'Don't you want to?'

'Not today.' She looked through the tiny fanning flames out to sea. This had been her chance to try and stop him going. But she didn't want to take it up. Not now. The day was too perfect.

'If we could always be here together . . .' He put some more wood on the fire.

She looked up at him. He looked so fantastic in the firelight. His slim dark body seemed to glow and there was a softness to his lips and his cheeks that she had hardly registered before.

'Do you want to?' he asked just as she was going to say the same thing. 'We never have,' he added.

'I want to,' she said. 'I really want to.'

'I brought something,' he said. 'We've got to be very careful.'

So he had calculated ahead, she thought. Matches. Contraceptives. What else had he planned?

'Where shall we do it?' he asked and she smiled; he looked like a little boy.

'Here,' said Sharon. 'In front of the fire.'

They just managed to catch the last train home, and as they sat in the chilly carriage they cuddled up together for body heat. Still she hadn't asked him; still she didn't want to. The day seemed gloriously endless; there was the rest of the railway journey and the walk home in the dark and the business of going to bed and sleeping and dreaming before she had to face the reality of the next day and all the battles she would have to face.

Then the miracle occurred.

'I've made up my mind,' said Imran, releasing her a little.

'Don't spoil it now.'

'I'm not spoiling anything.'

'What?' A terrible dangerous kind of joy seized her and she began to experience a shortness of breath that was not frightening but – something else. Something marvellous.

'It was good. What we did by the fire.'

'Yes.'

'I don't want anyone else to have that.'

'Are you sure?'

'Very sure. That's ours. No one else's. Right?'

'Right.'

'So I'm staying.'

Sharon suddenly felt like passing out; the whole train carriage swam in front of her eyes.

'What do you mean?' she said. It was too good to believe. Far too good.

'I'm not going to Pakistan. I'm not going anywhere. I'm staying with you. And to hell with Mick.'

Nine

Ever since he had seen his father talking to Mick, Leroy had been feeling more and more uneasy. Every spare moment he had kept wondering about it and the conversation they had had down by the canal. He would do anything to keep his father out of trouble, even to the extent of giving up his job on the Gallopers. But clearly his father did not want it, and perhaps was already on to something else. Leroy hoped to God that it did not have anything to do with Mick.

Luckily he didn't have many spare moments for most of his time was occupied with relentlessly polishing and in some cases carefully painting the horses. Jim had decided that some of the lettering needed attention again and he had got a sign writer to come and touch up the glowing colours. Soon the fair would move on to Clapham Common and Gallopers was going with it, so in the very little spare time he had left Leroy walked the old railway track with Gallica. The weather was still very fine; the Indian Summer was lasting although the nights were drawing in.

As they walked she said, 'I'll get down and see you at Clapham. Just as much.'

'Great,' he said and kissed her. He longed to confide in her but somehow felt he couldn't, out of loyalty to his father.

'You heard the latest?' she asked.

'I don't hear anything,' said Leroy. 'I'm too busy to hear anything.'

'Imran's not going to Pakistan after all.'

'I never believed he was. What's he going to do? Stay home and kill Mick?'

'He's going to avoid Mick the best he can. Aren't you pleased?'

'Sure. But I don't know him. I only met him a few days ago.'

She looked subdued and he was immediately sorry. He told her so and put his arm round her to reassure her.

'What's the matter?' she asked after a long silence.

'Nothing.'

'You're worried about something.'

In a burst of confidence he told her.

'He might just have been having a chat with him.'

'That yob and my dad? Come off it.' Leroy was incredulous. 'What have they got in common?'

She had to admit that on the surface they had very little.

'It really worries me,' he went on. 'Dad's got no work and neither has Mick. And Dad's getting desperate.'

'He wouldn't want to get mixed up with Mick. You don't know him. He's a moron.'

'It really worries me,' Leroy repeated.

Later, when she had left him, Gallica walked home, a bit concerned that Leroy was so absorbed with his own affairs. He never asked her about anything – like her parents or her African background. Wasn't he interested? she wondered.

Mick reached for the telephone as he lay on his bed. The extension had been in his room when they bought the house and his father had never got round to taking it out, although he had often threatened to do so.

'It's Gerry,' said the whispered voice.

'What are you whispering about?' asked Mick, sitting up and lighting a cigarette, flicking the match into an already full ashtray.

'Derek's around and I don't want him to know anything about this.'

'What do you want?'

'The job's tomorrow night. I want you to be in the car park underneath the flats at just after midnight. Just behind the back entrance. Do you know where that is?'

'Yeah.'

'Come alone. There'll be some other kids there. Just hang around with them till I come. And whatever you do, don't attract attention.'

'What about the money?'

'Half before you start and the rest when you've finished.'

'How long will it take?'

'Few minutes if you work at it.'

'What are we working at?'

'I'll tell you when I see you. I'll give everyone a general briefing, and Mick – '

'Yeah?'

'Don't tell anyone. If you want to work for me again keep quiet. Yes?'

'Sure. You mean there could be more work like whatever it is?'

'More work. Yeah.'

Mick put the phone down. He felt faintly uneasy. Why was the guy always so mysterious? Whatever he had in mind must be against the law. Mick thought of the money and felt better, although he still hadn't the slightest idea of what he might do with it. Get some slag and go to the South of France had been his most recent ill-formed idea. As he lay back blearily planning, Mick still found it impossible to throw off the sense of uneasiness. He couldn't bear to be locked up and because of that minor, previous offence he might well be if he was caught. What could Gerry be planning? Suddenly the thought of the offer Mr Dapor had made him came into his mind. He still burned with suspicious anger whenever he thought about it. That was their way of getting him in their power. Quite why he disliked the Dapors so much he had never really worked out, but it was something to do with their closeness and their success. Together they had built up their supermarket while his family had never worked together on anything. And now they had used his own sister as an intermediary to offer him their rotten little job. What cheek!

Sharon and Imran sat in the same Wimpy Bar they had sat in a couple of days ago when her spirits had been at their most hopeless and Imran had been at his most intractable. But now all that had changed and it seemed to be part of a distant past. They were both so happy now, so exultant in their own company and own decisions. The memory of the cave and the firelight and what they had done held a magical quality; it was a bond between them.

'When can we do it again?' said Imran suddenly.

'What?' She gaped stupidly at him. 'D'you mean make love?'

'You do want to, don't you?'

'You know I do.' She smiled at him.

'Well, when?'

'It's not a question of when. It's where.'

'The railway?'

'Anyone could come.'

'The car park?'

She hesitated. 'It's pretty squalid, but I reckon it's the only place we could go. And besides – we'll be together. And that's the important thing.'

'I could find a blanket. We could make a love nest.'

Sharon hesitated again. Was it just because of their love making that Imran had decided not to go to Pakistan? Quickly she dismissed the thought.

'Do you want to or not?' asked Imran impatiently.
'Yes,' said Sharon hastily. She thought again of the flames and the sea and sighed. But you couldn't always have it so good. She would just have to imagine it.

Gerry's desire for revenge on the Norths had increased as the days went past. He was so absorbed in it that the new ride took slow shape, despite Derek's help. Certainly he was a big advantage, but as Gerry had not really thought through the final concept they had had to start again at least a dozen times. He sensed that Derek was losing faith in him, despite the money. It really was true his aunt had left him money: only a couple of grand but enough to pay Derek and take care of the other little job. She had been close to him, had dear old Auntie Wendy. With no kids of her own she had doted on him and he had always liked her. She'd been a fortune-teller on Hastings Pier in the summer and had seen private clients in the winter. He'd never realised she'd made such a bomb. But this was his only bit of luck. There had been no more, particularly with the Guild. They had contacted him only yesterday, telling him that his new ride would be rigorously inspected and that an enquiry was being held into the accident in conjunction with the police. Gerry knew for sure that Jim North had put the boot in for him. Well, he would pay him back and he wouldn't have long to wait.
He wandered out of the lean-to workshop into the

bleak muddy field that was littered with similar shacks. In fact it was like a shanty town with its trailers and tumble-down buildings and bits of rusting fairground machinery. A vast trelliswork of metal was scattered over the mud, partly protected with tattered sheets of polythene.

Derek, who was welding over the far side, ignored Gerry's presence as best he could. The only good thing that he could think of was that he was losing weight. Fast. Still, once he had completed the job, which would probably take another couple of weeks, he would take the money and run.

Gerry wandered towards his trailer.

'How long's that going to take?' he snapped.

''Bout half an hour.'

'That's too long.'

Derek had never heard Gerry sound so impatient, but he shrugged, understanding the pressure he was under. In a way he felt sorry for him, but as he pulled his welding mask over his face, Derek quickly forgot him.

'This'll be your first pull-down,' said Jim to Leroy.

'What's it like?'

'Hell. The whole lot's got to come down tomorrow night, be stacked on the truck and set up again at Clapham by the next afternoon. We used to find it tough enough with Derek.'

Gwen stepped out of the trailer and overheard the last few words. 'Derek?' She laughed. 'Derek was either drunk or complaining that he had something wrong with him. Something that would stop him lifting. You're going to be a bonus, Leroy.'

Jim smiled. 'I reckon I'm being too hard on you, son. Gwen's right. You're a bonus all round.' He gave him a mock punch on the arm and Leroy felt a warm glow of content. He had never been so happy. Then the shadow of Mick and his dad crossed the back of his mind and he shuddered.

'Someone walk over your grave?' Gwen asked.

'Something like that,' replied Leroy.

'It's awful.' Sharon looked around her anxiously.

'Not so bad,' muttered Imran. He had put a couple of blankets down in a far corner of the disused underground garage that ran all the way under Starling Point.

When the complex was first built, Starling Point residents had parked their cars there but inevitably there was vandalism. Now only a few tried to use it. Derelict cars littered the broken concrete floor. Wan moonlight filtered through the empty space. There was a taxi with no wheels and enough old chairs and sofas to furnish a couple of large houses. Half of the floor was filled with pools of rainwater and an eternal gloom filled the place. Local kids called it the Fortress. It certainly looked like one in a broken-down sort of way for the council had surrounded the entrance and exit with steel fencing, some of which had been pulled down and never replaced. Occasionally the wind penetrated the Fortress and, when it was in a certain direction, worming its way through the partly boarded-up entrance, it moaned and howled in the huge dark cavern. Local mythology called it the cry of the werewolf.

'We can't stay here,' said Sharon very positively.

'No?' Imran said quietly.

Well, she thought, the romance has certainly gone out of this and once again she was reminded of her former fears – that he only wanted her for her body.

'It's so squalid.'

'But private.'

Imran put his arms round her and they lay on the blankets. Sharon shivered and he squeezed her tighter.

'I'll make you warm,' he said.

'I love you,' she breathed into his ear. Suddenly the pressure of his body reassured her and she forgot both her surroundings and her suspicions. Sharon closed her eyes; she could smell the sea and watch the flickering flames at the mouth of the cave.

They must have been asleep for over an hour when Sharon was suddenly awakened by Imran, who had put his hand over her mouth. She struggled and he breathed urgently into her ear, 'Don't move.'

For a moment she was still on the ride at the fair. The car had come off the tracks and was dangling over the abyss. 'Don't move,' Imran had said and he was saying it again now. She froze and distantly heard voices. Straining her ears she recognised one as her brother's.

'When?' he was asking. 'When?'

''Bout an hour.'

Other voices came in and out swimmily. They were speaking softly but the great vault around them seemed to magnify the whispers.

'What we meant to do?'

'Hang around. He'll be here soon.'

'What we doing? Robbing a bank or something?'

It was Mick's voice again and Sharon could detect that he was afraid.

'He said to wait.'

One of the voices was slurred and she realised that they had all been drinking. Then she heard footsteps and Imran tightened his grip on her arm.

'Everyone here?' The voice was brisk and authoritative and was answered by a variety of suspicious mutterings. Sharon could hear someone drinking out of a can.

'What have we got to do?' asked Mick.

Sharon and Imran lay there in the darkness, not daring to speak or move. Yes, thought Sharon. It's almost the same as being in the overhanging car. Maybe worse. She looked at Imran in the gloom. He mouthed at her to be quiet.

'All right, lads. I'll tell you what I want you to do once we're outside. And I'll pay you half now and half when the job's done.'

There was a muffled cheer and the stamping of feet. Then silence.

'Where are they?'

Imran took her in his arms. 'I don't care where they are. They've gone.'

'But what's Mick up to? It sounds dodgy.'

'To hell with him.'

'I must find out. Besides, they may come back.'

'It's always the same, isn't it?' His voice had taken on a hard and bitter note.

'What is?'

'You always put Mick first.'

'Rubbish.'

'Then what are you doing now?'

'He's in trouble.'

'Mick's always in trouble.'

'I'm going to follow them.'

'No.'

'I've got to.'

'What can you do?'

'Stop him.'

'They'll kill you.'

Sharon got up. 'I'll see you later.'

'I'll come with you.' Imran got to his feet as well.

Sharon shivered in the chilly space around them. 'You don't have to,' she said. As she spoke she knew that Mick's intrusion into their lives again could well be fatal. But much as she would like to, she couldn't desert him now.

Immediately they crept out of the car park entrance they could hear the shouting and smashing. The sound was terrible – like a massacre. Their voices were hoarse with insult and what they were yelling made her shudder. Then she saw them under the light of the jaundiced moon, gathered around the Gallopers. At first she could not believe what she was seeing, then she began to scream, bellowing in Imran's face:

'They're cutting the heads off the horses. Can't you see? They're cutting off their heads!'

Ten

It was the twins who were wakened by the noise first and they soon alerted Jim and Gwen.

'What the hell's going on?' Jim rolled out of bed and hit the floor with a thump.

'Dad,' said Dan, 'someone's hurting the horses.'

'What?' He and Gwen could hear the noise now.

'I'm going out there,' said Gwen, but Jim was by the door already, wrenching it open and pushing her back.

'Stay here,' he yelled. 'And keep the kids in.'

Sharon and Jim arrived by the roundabout at exactly the same time. They stood before it, unable to take in what was happening. The damage was appalling. Six of the freshly painted horses were headless – and on the ground in front of them lay the wildly grinning heads, golden manes glinting wickedly in the moonlight. The gang were on the other side of the roundabout now, axes held high, locked in hesitation. Mick was standing nearest to her, looking at the weapon in his hand as if he was surprised.

'What are you doing?' she whispered. 'What in God's name are you doing?'

He looked back at her with dull, unresponding eyes. Sharon turned away to see one of the gang beginning to run for it. With a cry of sheer animal rage, Jim threw himself at the boy. The axe dropped from his hand as they fell to the ground and landed by one of the severed heads.

'You bastard!' Jim was sitting on the boy, raining blows on him, while Gwen stood on the steps yelling her head off. She charged down towards them and the terrified gang turned and fled, though not before one of them had karate-kicked Jim in the head as he ran past. Imran was beside her now, moving towards Mick, his fists clenched. But he stopped when he saw Jim topple forward.

Mick ran, following the others, and soon there was total silence in the square. Jim lay still with Imran beside him. Gwen was a little way away, frozen to the spot.

Then, with the guttural cry of an animal in pain, Gwen broke the strange tableau. She went to her husband's side, closely followed by the sobbing twins, and knelt beside him and Imran. Curiously, they looked as if they were all in prayer.

Mick, said Sharon somewhere deep inside herself. What have you done?

Leroy was woken by the sound of police sirens. Running to the window he looked down at the fairground. A shadow was lying beside the roundabout, bathed in moonlight, and figures were standing around it. There were two tiny shapes that kept darting about and Leroy suddenly recognised them as the twins. A chill touched his heart as he continued to stare down. He was sure the pallid light was distorting what he saw, for the blotched and shifting night made it look as if some of the Gallopers were headless.

'Dad,' he yelled out. 'Dad, come quick.'

When his father did not appear Leroy ran into the bedroom and found only his mother blearily awake. The other side of the bed was empty and the chill inside him turned to ice.

'That's all we can tell you,' said Sharon as she sat in the police car between Imran and the community policeman, Reg. They had known him for many years and had always felt safe with him. Reg was trusted at Starling Point. He knew everyone and he helped run a junior football league. Over the years he had slowly built up both respect and affection.

'And Mick? Where's he gone, do you reckon?' His voice was soft, confiding.

She shrugged. 'God knows. Not home, anyway.' Tears filled her eyes and Imran put his arm round her.

'He'll be back,' he said.

Sharon closed her eyes. 'What will they get?' she asked Reg.

He shrugged. 'Depends what happens to Jim North, doesn't it?'

* * *

Leroy was trying to comfort the twins when his father arrived, striding out of the darkness, his jacket torn and his eyes fierce. Shock waves passed through Leroy as he wondered where he had been. Finally he plucked up enough courage to ask.

'None of your damned business,' his dad rapped out in the old way. He looked down at the twins, pathetically sitting on the trailer steps, staring fixedly at the grinning heads. Sebastian's eyes softened. 'What are you two doing out in the cold?'

'We're waiting for our mum,' said Dan.

'Dad's not well,' murmured Sally.

'He's going to be fine.' Sebastian looked down at the horses' heads as if for the first time. 'What the hell's going on here?' he asked. When Leroy had explained, Sebastian said, 'You mean Mick was in on this?'

'So they say.'

He looked away and Leroy wondered what he was thinking.

'Come on,' said Sebastian, walking up the steps of the trailer and grabbing the twins by their hands. 'I'm going to read you a story.'

The twins looked at Leroy doubtfully.

'He's a great storyteller,' he said, not looking his dad in the eye for he had never read him a story in his life.

'It's never too late to start,' Sebastian pronounced, disappearing into the trailer with the twins.

* * *

The grey light of dawn found a small crowd standing around the Gallopers. A couple of policemen stood guard on the roundabout while others were out looking for the members of the gang.

The residents of Starling Point were sombre, shattered by what had happened. A milk float had stopped and the milkman was staring down at the six severed heads. The painted smiles were mocking and a small newspaper boy turned away, tears in his eyes. The quiet pathos of the horses' heads was riveting, and most of the crowd were unable to take their eyes off them, particularly as they had already heard on the grapevine that Jim North was fighting for his life.

Sharon and Imran were eventually taken home by the police and, while Sebastian tried to distract the wailing twins inside the trailer, Leroy stood in front of the roundabout staring down unbelievingly at the carnage. A couple of press photographers had just arrived and were now flooding the frozen drama with cameras and flashlights. Leroy's eyes filled with tears and he wept for Jim and Gwen and the twins and all his own shattered dreams. They wouldn't be able to keep him on now. The selfish thought kept beating at his mind and the tears kept flowing. Another, even more desperate thought, kept stabbing at Leroy. Had his father had anything to do with this? Why had he been talking to Mick those nights ago? And why had he been out of the house last night, arriving with his jacket all torn. The questions continued to torment Leroy until he could bear them no longer. Unable to keep looking at the smiling heads, he went round the back of the trailer and cried his heart out.

'You done what?' Derek was incredulous as he stared at a triumphant Gerry across the scrubby meadow.

'I've taught him a lesson,' Gerry said grinning as he walked across the mud. 'I've smashed up his ride. That'll teach him. Perhaps he'll keep off my back now.'

'You smashed Gallopers?' whispered Derek. He just could not believe what Gerry was saying. He must be lying. He must.

'Well, not myself like. I hired the local mafiosa.'

'What did they do?' Derek's voice was soft and menacing but Gerry did not notice his tone. He was elated, jubilant.

'I had some of the nags cut off in their prime and . . .'

Derek strode forward and grabbed Gerry round the throat. He reeled back, amazed and indignant.

'You did *what*?' Derek repeated again, staring into Gerry's eyes with increasing fury.

'I told you,' Gerry spluttered. 'Get off.'

'You know the value of them horses?'

Gerry made an inarticulate sound.

'You know you can't insure them?' Derek released Gerry and belted him as hard as he knew how. As Gerry rolled in the mud Derek shouted, 'You're an animal – just an animal!'

'You can consider our partnership at an end,'

gasped Gerry, staggering to his feet. 'And you won't get your money.'

'I don't want it.' Derek grabbed Gerry again, this time by his jacket.

'You hit me again and I'll get the Old Bill on you,' he whined.

'That's just where you're going,' said Derek firmly. 'But we're making another call first.'

Derek found himself shaking with shock and hatred. He knew Gerry was a born loser, knew that he was a fantasy merchant who had very little grasp of reality. But he had not realised how vindictive he was. Derek closed his eyes, blinking back the tears. He had never known how much he really loved the Gallopers. The thought of the horses broken and mutilated made him want to beat the wretched, inadequate, hopelessly childish Gerry right into the ground.

Sharon's conversation with her parents was not as bad as she was expecting. They seemed stunned, numb to what Mick had done, to the fact that he was missing. They both sat and looked like frightened children and Sharon suddenly felt a responsibility for them that she had never felt before. But the fact that she had spent the night in the Fortress with Imran seemed to shock them even more.

'How *could* you do it?' asked her mother over and over again while her father, grim-faced and silent, accused her with his eyes. He looked at her as if she was a personal treasure that had been broken or sullied in some way. But when she told them that Jim North was in hospital, their numb bewilderment turned to acute anxiety.

Why couldn't they have supported Mick better in the past? she thought angrily. All they had done was to write him off and what had happened was a predictable enough reaction on his part.

'Mick will go down for this,' said her father, closing his eyes. Her mother began to cry. They really *were* like children, Sharon thought, trying to adjust to the reversal of their relationship. Just then the telephone rang and she ran to answer it, thinking that it was Imran but praying that it might be Mick.

It was Leroy. 'I thought I'd phone you and tell you the latest on Jim.'

She was immediately grateful. 'Thanks. Is he – ?' Leroy's voice shook. 'They don't know if he's going to live, Sharon. Whoever hit him on the head hit him mighty hard.'

When she rang off, Sharon told her parents what Leroy had said. Her father left the room and ran upstairs to his bedroom while her mother continued to weep noisily. Suddenly Sharon felt very old.

At Imran's house the emotional temperature began at a lower pitch. He was alone with his father, his mother and Naveed having been excluded from the conversation.

'So you were driven to spend the night in the car park with her.' His father's voice was sad.

'There was nowhere else to go.'

'You could not have come here.' He shook his head as if arguing with himself. 'You have offended against our faith,' he added slowly.

'Don't give me that or I'll get out now,' yelled Imran.

'I am only saying what I believe.'

Suddenly Imran wanted to shake his father. 'I can do without it,' he said miserably.

'Have you been with her?'

'I've slept with her,' said Imran reluctantly.

His father shook his head again. 'I am too much in both worlds myself. It is my fault.' It was as if he was thinking aloud. 'Ever since we came here I have tried to have a foot in the West and a foot in the East. It's no good; I should have stayed with Islam.'

'The roundabout man. He was hurt bad,' said Imran urgently.

His father tried to pull himself together. 'I offered that Mick a job,' he said vaguely, leaving his armchair and pacing about. His thoughts seemed disconnected and he was obviously completely distraught.

Imran suddenly felt deeply concerned for his father. He could understand his dilemma, understand how liberal he had been – and that now he was bitterly regretting stepping outside Islam. He went over, and kissed him on the forehead.

'I don't want to see you suffer, Father.'

'I *should* suffer.'

'I don't want that.'

Mr Dapor got up and walked slowly to the door.

It was early in the morning and he was still in his dressing gown.

'Where are you going?'

'I am going to the mosque,' he said. 'Please wait for me here.'

'No.'

'Very well.' His father shrugged. 'I cannot beat you. You are too big.'

'I want to come with you, Father.'

'What? To the mosque?'

Imran took his father's hand. 'I want us to go together.'

After speaking to Sharon, Leroy ran straight to the hospital. A nurse directed him to the ward but in the corridor he paused. Gwen's huddled figure was on the bench outside. Leroy sat down beside her and after a while she looked up.

'Jim's going to die,' she whispered. 'The doctor says that he's going to die.' She buried her face in Leroy's jerkin. Leroy stroked her long, dark hair and thought of his father.

'Let's pray for him,' was all he could think of saying, and in a mumbling kind of way Gwen began to recite the Lord's Prayer.

The mosque was small and quite empty. A few streets away from Starling Point, it had been specially built many years ago. Now it was shabby and crouched in the shadow of a huge D.I.Y. warehouse on a strip of patchy grass where the faithful used to prostrate themselves in the summer. Inside there was an increased feeling of shabbiness. The interior was plain with simply a copy of the Qur'an and a large number of prayer mats.

Imran and his father took off their shoes at the door and went and knelt on the carpet. Imran had not been there for a long time and suddenly he felt relaxed. His father lowered his head to the floor and began to pray. Imran closed his eyes and the rhythmic cadences of his father's prayers seemed to sweep him away to a place where his life took meaning. It was an extraordinary sensation, invigorating and illuminating at the same time.

Derek parked the battered old van outside the hospital and turned to Gerry who was sitting hunched up in the passenger seat.

'Look, I don't want to go through with this.'

'You'll do it or I'll break your arm. Just in case you get the idea of doing a bunk you have to remember that you have left all your worldly goods in Chertsey and I know where they are. So you won't be going anywhere, will you?'

'No,' said Gerry. 'I won't.'

As they walked out of the mosque, Imran looked at his watch and saw that it was almost nine o'clock. He stared at his father. It was unheard-of for him not to be in the supermarket at eight whatever happened. Having broken the habit of a lifetime he sat down on a seat outside the mosque.

'You should be at work, Dad,' said Imran wonderingly. He still felt detached, away from the real world. Why had this happened? he wondered. Why was he suddenly feeling so full of purpose?

'I'm not going to work today, son. The business can look after itself. Your mother and Naveed and the staff will cope.'

'What are you going to do?'

'I have prayed.'

'Yes?'

'And I have been given guidance.'

He was silent and Imran waited. He didn't want to hurry him. He remembered how his father had been guided before when they were children and how change had emerged. Like taking his mother for a holiday, or discovering how unhappy Naveed was at the Primary School, or preventing his uncle from going bankrupt. What was going to happen now?

'You will be welcome to bring Sharon to our house.'

'*What*?' Imran felt the world rocking about him.

'On the strict understanding that you have no more sex. That you wait for that until you are married.'

Imran had no idea what to say. But his father did not seem to need reassurance.

'There is more. When this Mick is found I want you to know that the job is still on offer to him.'

'He won't take it,' said Imran gloomily.

'I said the offer is still there. Now, there is more.'

'Yes?'

'This man. This Jim North. How bad is he?'

'I don't know. I can find out.'

'He is a good man. He took on an apprentice. He has been good to him. I hear this on the grapevine.'

'It's certainly public knowledge.' Imran met his father's eyes.

'The apprentice – the boy whose father was in prison.'

'Yes.'

'This man North is outside our community but has done us a good turn. Therefore he should be rewarded.'

'How?'

'His horses were damaged. They were the pride of his life, I gather. Do you remember Mr Mahood?'

'The old woodcarver?'

'He has made statues for the mosque in London. He is very good. He would do a fast job on the horses. He could repair and renew.'

'For the love of it?'

'I would pay him.'

Imran stared at his father unbelievingly.

'You see,' continued his father in further explanation, 'I have been guided.'

Imran leant forward and kissed him. 'You are a very good man, Father.'

'I am a man who prays and who is reminded of his own community responsibility. And by that I do not mean the Pakistani community. We are all as one at Starling Point. We have to be. Do we not?'

'If you say so, Father.' Imran grinned.

'I do say so.' He rose to his feet. 'At first I thought I had to return to Eastern ways. But now I know what I have to do. I am going to the hospital. I wish to speak to Mr North.'

'What the hell do you two want?' Gwen looked up furiously at Derek and Gerry.

'I've come to help,' said Derek. He stood there in front of her awkwardly, like a child owning up.

'Push off!' Gwen turned away.

'Gerry is going to pay for the damage. Aren't you?'

Gerry nodded but Gwen looked away again as if she couldn't bear them anywhere near her. Derek stared at her hopelessly.

'You walked out on us, Derek. Don't expect to come back. You was replaced.' She glanced at Leroy and Derek winced.

'Please, Gwen – '

She shrugged. 'It's all too late now. I'm not taking you back whatever you say.'

'I'm not asking you to – '

But he was interrupted by the arrival of Imran and his father.

Mr Dapor looked agitated. 'We had a job getting in,' he said. 'They said we were not relatives. I managed to be persuasive.'

'This is a bad time,' said Gwen. 'Don't talk to me now. Why don't you *all* clear off?'

Mr Dapor looked at her determinedly. 'I have been guided by my prayers and I have come to make your husband an offer.'

'We don't know if Jim's going to live,' choked Gwen. 'I don't want to hear about any offers.'

But Mr Dapor ploughed on. 'I shall employ a craftsman.'

'What for?'

'To repair your galloping horses.'

'You'd need an expert to do that.'

'I *have* an expert and I will pay him. Your husband has done much for our community.'

'But he's never had anything to do with your community.'

'My dear Mrs North, I do not mean *our* community. I mean *our* community.'

She was staring at him as if he was crazy and Imran noticed that all the others were also gazing at him as if he had gone stark raving mad.

'Permit me to explain,' continued Mr Dapor, 'I can see there is a misunderstanding.' He turned back to Gwen. 'You and your husband brought joy to our community. And by that I mean Starling Point – the community to which we all belong.' He gestured towards Leroy. 'You gave this boy a job when he needed it most.'

But Gwen was not even listening.

'It's too late,' she said again. 'My husband is dying.' And she burst into a great wail of anguish.

The young doctor walked down the corridor and frowned as he saw the crowd outside the ward. These fairground people, he thought. They shouldn't all be here like this. Black, brown, white, gypsy-like.

'Mrs North.'

Gwen looked up at him beseechingly. 'Yes?'

'Will you step this way?'

Eleven

Mick had gone to his secret place but, as he sat opposite the old lady, he knew it would only be a matter of time before they found him. He had been coming here for some months, unbeknown to anyone, ever since he had picked her up from where she had fallen in the street. Mick could never really explain to himself why he had helped her. At the time he was deeply depressed, had never felt so miserable, but staggering up the walkway afterwards and then into the lift had given him a faint glow – a glow that increased as he continued to visit her.

Because of the help he had given her, Mrs Willard seemed to trust him completely and, more importantly, to respect him. Soon Mick found himself talking freely to her about his problems. She never made any attempt to advise him but she did listen. She made him tea, and gave him home-made cakes and planned little treats and surprises for him. He had always resented grown-ups, particularly those who tried to give him advice, but with the old lady it was different. She rarely went out. The flat was overrun with cats and there was a nasty shut-in smell to the whole place. But he kept on going, kept on talking to her, kept on eating her little treats. Slowly the flat became home to him: the home he had never had.

Sometimes Mick would arrive and not want to talk and they would quietly watch the television together. A cup of tea would magically appear at his elbow, a little cake or some chocolate biscuits on a plate. Once she had kissed him, feathery light on his cheek. At other times she would talk of her life with her husband in Africa. She said that he had been a big game hunter. Mick had no idea how true this was but really the truth didn't matter. Slowly he became very fond of her and would sometimes help her in the flat. Mick had found his sanctuary and he jealously guarded it as a secret. He told none of his mates. No one. He wanted to keep it as a secret place of his own, where he was loved and wanted, where he could be himself and where no one ever asked any questions – except the right ones.

Mrs Willard had accepted him immediately when he had arrived in the early morning, hobbling to the door, reassured by his voice, unlocking his sanctuary. He had told her what had happened and she had nodded, making tea and sitting with him, not advising him, not asking him to make a decision.

'I didn't touch his horses. I didn't touch *him*.'

She had comforted him, holding his hand as if he were a frightened child. If only he could stay here forever, he thought. If only he could stay in the tiny crowded room for the rest of his life. A huge cat moved on to his lap, the television set flickered, he ate buttered toast. Mick knew he was deliberately blocking the rest of the world out. But for how long?

Gwen walked slowly back to the bench and Leroy, Derek, Gerry, Imran and Mr Dapor stared at her in concern. But then they saw the smile on her face. It was an unbelieving sort of smile but it was there. Leroy breathed a sigh of relief.

'He's going to be all right!' Gwen sat down heavily and burst into tears. But this time they were tears of happiness. 'The doctor says he's going to pull through. He's got a skull fracture but it's not as bad as they thought and he's not going to have brain damage and . . .'

'I have been praying,' said Mr Dapor rather proudly.

'Can we see him?' asked Leroy. He felt overwhelmed with a sense of relief. But the worry about his father was still there, burning away.

'Not yet. Not even me. But this afternoon, he said. Later this afternoon.'

Leroy stood up and gently propelled Gwen to her feet. 'We must go back to the twins,' he said.

'We're going down the nick,' said Derek. Gerry nodded dumbly.

'May I return with you?' Mr Dapor asked Gwen. 'I would like to see the extent of the damage.'

'You're welcome,' said Gwen, suddenly throwing her arms around Mr Dapor and kissing him. 'You're our guardian angel.'

Mr Dapor emerged from her embrace extremely flustered. 'I am doing what is right,' he said. 'That is all.'

Imran grinned.

'Dad – '

Sebastian was sitting on the steps of the trailer while Gwen and Mr Dapor examined the decapitated horses. The twins jumped around them, jubilant at the news of their father.

'Yeah?' He looked exhausted.

'What were you talking to Mick about?' Leroy was trembling as he looked down at his father, but whether it was from fatigue or fear he couldn't tell.

'Mick?'

'I saw you talking to him. Couple of nights ago.'

'So?'

'I just want to know.' Leroy's voice was so indistinct that his father could hardly hear him.

Sebastian looked down at the horses' heads and then back at Leroy. 'You think I had something to do with all this?' His voice was expressionless.

'You came here with your jacket all torn,' said Leroy in passionate bewilderment.

'That was from my job.'

'But you haven't got a job.'

'I didn't tell you. But I offered Mick the same chance.'

Leroy stared at him bewilderedly. 'What chance?'

Sebastian sighed. 'It ain't much of a job and I don't reckon it's going to last, so I told your mum to keep it quiet like. But it's money and I thought Mick would need some too. I'm not proud. I don't care what I do nowadays, providing it's straight.'

Leroy felt he was going to scream with frustration at any moment. 'Dad – *what* job?'

Sebastian grinned. 'I'm a bouncer, son. Down at the Fantasy Club. That's how I got me jacket ripped – bit of hustle last night. There were a couple of bouncer jobs going so I offered one to young Mick. But no takers.'

'Why didn't you tell me earlier?'

Sebastian looked away. 'You've got prospects, son. I've got none. That's why.'

Suddenly Leroy felt he could shout with joy and then shame swept over him. Why hadn't he trusted him?

'Dad, you can have this job. I'm sure Jim and . . .'

'I told you before. No. Now, where is young Mick?'

'He's gone missing.'

'So he's mixed up in this, is he?'

'Looks like it.'

Sebastian got to his feet. 'I'm going to look for him. He won't have gone far. But he'll be dangerous now. Back to the wall with nowhere to go.'

'I'm sorry, Dad.'

'What about?'

'I doubted you.'

'That's not surprising.' He got up quickly. 'I'll go look for Mick.'

'Can I come with you?'

'No way. That boy's trouble.'

'We been through trouble before. Together.'

'This is dangerous.'

'So was the Mystery Ride. We were together in that.'

Sebastian shook his head. 'It's not the same. This kid's in a lot of trouble, Leroy. It's best he doesn't start any more. I know what it's like. One thing leads to another and . . .' He looked away. Then he got up and began to walk towards the piazza.

'Dad – ' called Leroy, but his father did not look back.

Gerry and Derek were sitting outside the nick. Gerry was desperate, knowing that he was pleading an impossible case.

'Give me a chance, for God's sake.'

'Get inside. Go on – before I give you another one.'

'Please – ' Gerry's voice quavered. 'I'll pay every penny back to him.'

'He doesn't need it now. The local do-gooder's got him.'

'I'll set *us* up then. You can be boss.'

'I wouldn't work with you if you paid me a fortune. You're a small-time crook who's going nowhere.'

But Gerry could see the inside of a cell. He made one last desperate effort. 'I'll go straight. I'll make a safe ride.'

'You're not capable of either. Besides, you're bound to be nicked sooner or later. One of them kids will grass you up when they get hold of them.'

Gerry then grasped at a straw. 'My old man – he always knew I was no good. I had to try it on me own and, OK, he was right. I've blown it. But if you give me a chance, Derek, I'll change that ride. I mean we'd hardly started, had we?'

'That's because – '

'I know. It's my fault. But look, suppose I drop the big stuff?'

'What big stuff?'

'Supposing I make a kiddies' ride? Something harmless. Something that can't go wrong. None of your super-rides. I make it. You help me. Then you run it.'

Derek stared at him cynically. 'I don't believe you,' he said.

'I'll prove it. I promise.'

Derek paused again. He was almost tempted to believe him and for a few seconds he thought of Gerry's money and how useful it would be. Then he realised how stupid the temptation really was. The money would soon run out and whatever he did with Gerry was bound to end in disaster.

'No,' he said.

'Please . . .' Gerry's eyes were on the blue lamp. Then they were on Derek: hopeful, pleading, ingratiating eyes. 'I'll do anything you say, Derek.'

The whine in his voice made Derek feel slightly sick but somehow he understood. However much he didn't like it, there were certain similarities between the two of them. Both had been smothered by their families. At least Gerry had broken away but he,

Derek, had only just escaped from Gwen. They would be a fatal combination together though, he thought.

'All right,' said Derek, suddenly decisive as he backed the van away from the police station. 'I'm not going to run you in.' As Gerry gazed at him gratefully he drove round the corner and stopped. 'Now get out.'

'Eh?'

'I said, get out. You'll be nicked sooner or later so I might as well give you some rope. But we're finished. Get it?'

Gerry got it and clambered out of the van as fast as he could in case Derek changed his mind. He hurried off down the street without looking back and Derek watched him go. Then he turned the van round and drove off in the opposite direction.

He didn't know where he was going, he had no idea what money he was going to earn, but he knew he could never go back to Gwen. It was a lonely, desperate start but he had to make it. Then Derek realised something. He was still driving Gerry's van. Well, that was a beginning. The van could be sold and provide him with some capital. Derek began to look for a second-hand car pitch.

Streets away, Gerry remembered the van and cursed. He didn't know what was going to happen to him either but, unlike Derek, Gerry had an imagination. As he walked he began to plan.

'I've got some good news.' Gwen proceeded to tell Jim about Mr Dapor's offer. 'This Mr Dapor's already been to see the horses. If his friend works flat out, he reckons he can have them repaired in a fortnight. Well in time for Covent Garden.'

'Blimey,' was all Jim could say but she could see the joy in his eyes. He looked as if a miracle had just happened. He tried to turn his head and winced with the pain.

'Leroy.'

'Yeah?'

'Come into vision.'

Leroy moved round the bed so that Jim could see him.

'You still want to work for me?'

'You know I do.' There was an awkward pause. 'But what about Derek?'

'What about him?'

'He could be a lot more use to you than me.'

'Derek's a good mechanic and he's got the strength of a rhino.'

'So there you are then.'

'He's also deserted us. I'd never have him back. And he knows it.'

'He's going to nick Gerry,' said Gwen.

'I don't care what he does – he's not coming back.'

'I never said he was.'

'I've got my partner.' Jim stretched out a hand to Leroy and Leroy took it.

'Gallopers will be even better when it's repaired,' said Leroy. 'You see if it isn't.'

'We're heading for the big time, Jim. Covent

Garden and on from there.' Gwen stroked his forehead. 'We're going to be all right.'

Jim grinned. 'With a couple of partners like you two, how could I go wrong?'

Sharon and Imran were sitting in the Dapors' front room. They sat on opposite sides of the settee and an old Pakistani lady sat between them.

'She doesn't understand English,' said Imran. 'She's a visiting aunt.'

'Do you have many visiting aunts?'

'Only in the mating season,' replied Imran. 'She is our protection. Or more likely, my father's.'

'She's our minder,' laughed Sharon.

'Do you object?'

'I don't have much choice. At least we can meet and talk here. It's warm. It's nice,' she added hurriedly.

Imran grinned at her. 'Maybe we can go to your house one day.'

'Maybe, but they're not thinking of anyone else but Mick at the moment.'

'Any news?'

'No.'

'He'll be OK.'

'He'll be scared stiff.' Her voice shook. 'Don't let's talk about him for a bit.' She looked across at Imran's aunt. 'Will she mind if we hold hands?'

'I don't think so.'

She took his hand, thinking of the cave and the firelight and the way their bodies had connected.

'You won't be going to Pakistan, then?' she said.

He shook his head. 'I'm getting round to believing what Dad believes in. We all have different ways. But in the end, we belong here. To Starling Point.'

She sighed with sudden contentment.

Imran squeezed her hand. 'Remember the cave?' he asked.

Mick was watching an evening game show when the knock came at the door. She winked at him as she got up, as if to say 'Don't worry, I'll keep you safe'.

When she opened the door, she knew she had failed him at once; his old denim jacket was sprawled over the chair and one of her cats was sitting on it. The black man stared at the jacket and then back at her.

'I think a young friend of mine is here.'

Mick thought about the jacket too, and as he got up he felt ready to fight for his freedom. But then he looked round the room and remembered where he was. The television set flickered, a flight of china swans climbed the wall, the kettle was singing and her cardigan was draped over the ironing board. He mustn't wreck his sanctuary; it might be waiting for him when he got back. Mick walked towards the door and she turned to him with eyes full of alarm.

'It's all right,' he reassured her. 'He's an old friend.'

'He'll look after you?' she quavered.

'Oh yes, he'll look after me all right.' He kissed her. 'See you soon,' he said.

'It will be soon?' she said, her hands plucking at the old denim jacket he was putting on.

Mick nodded. 'It will be soon,' he repeated.

'How did you find me?' asked Mick as they walked down the stairs.

'A process of elimination. I decided to knock at every door in Starling Point.'

'You must be knackered.'

'I am. Lucky I'd only done three blocks.'

'So what do I do now?'

'Give yourself up.'

'And what if I don't? What are you doing – making a citizen's arrest?'

'No. I'm giving you a piece of advice. How long you known the old lady?'

'None of your business. I wasn't doing her any harm.'

'I didn't say you were.'

'She's a friend of mine. Only one I got.' Mick paused on the stairs. 'So what if I do a bunk, then?'

'Do one.'

'You'll try and stop me.'

'No.'

'What's your game, then?'

'I was like you.'

'You're black.'

'Yes, but I was still like you.' Sebastian wasn't to be put off. 'No work. Doesn't matter about your colour if you got no work. Then I got some – and blew it by putting myself in trouble. Like I was telling you when I offered you that job.'

'I don't want to be no bouncer. Besides, *I* got the offer of a job.'

'What job?'

'In a supermarket.'

'Mr Dapor?'

'What of it?'

'Great. Go and see him before you go down the nick. Go and firm it up.'

Mick nodded. 'You're not taking me in, then?'

'I'm not taking you anywhere,' said Sebastian.

Gallica met Leroy just as he came out of the hospital.

'How's Jim?' she asked.

'He's getting on pretty well.'

She fell into step with him as they began to walk back to Starling Point.

'Leroy – '

'Yeah?'

'We'll still see each other, won't we?'

'You bet. We'll be in Covent Garden when the ride's fixed up. You can come up there – ' he paused and then hurried on a little too quickly – 'we'll see a lot of each other.' He sounded brisk and defensive.

Is this the beginning of the end? wondered Gallica, with sudden despondency. Then she buried the unpleasant thought, determined not to be so pessimistic.

'Yes,' she said. 'It'll be good.' They were silent as they continued walking. 'After all,' said Gallica, 'you could be at sea.'

'That's right,' replied Leroy, a little too readily.

'It'll work out all right.'
'You bet.'
Will it? wondered Gallica miserably. Will it? But she was determined not to let Leroy know what she was thinking. And so was he.

Mick saw the lights were still on in the supermarket and he walked slowly over to the entrance. Mr Dapor was just locking the door as he arrived. He looked alarmed to see him.
'Don't worry,' Mick said. 'I'm going down the nick to give myself up.'
'You are?' Mr Dapor stared doubtfully at him.
'But I wanted to ask you something first.'
'Yes?'
'It might go a bit better for me in court if I said that I had a job to go to. I don't suppose your offer's still on?'
Mr Dapor paused and stared at Mick. 'Of course it's still on,' he replied firmly. 'You can start when you like.'
'It might not be right away,' said Mick. 'But thanks, I'd like it.'
As Mick left the supermarket he felt a hand on his shoulder. It was not a friendly one. He found himself being spun round, then he was looking into the furious face of Imran.
'What the hell have you been doing to my dad?'
Mick stared back at him. It would be great to beat him to a pulp. But how could he now?
'What's going on?' Sharon ran up behind Imran.

'I reckon he's been threatening my dad. Calling him a Paki or something.'

But Mr Dapor was already at the door. 'You are jumping to conclusions.'

'What?'

'Michael is going to give himself up. He came to ask me, with great courtesy, if my offer of a job will still be open. In a while. And of course I told him that it very definitely would be.'

'Blimey,' was all that Imran could say but Sharon came up and flung her arms round her brother.

'Welcome home,' she said.